# My Tattered Bonds

## The Bloodstone Saga

By
Courtney Cole

ISBN-13: 978-0615574653

## DEDICATION

To my husband, my daughter and my sons.
Thank you for putting up with me during the many different
worlds that I write about.
Know this:
No matter what world I create in my books,
I will always, always prefer to live in mine,
with you.

# Chapter One

The girl's skin glistened in the firelight. She was ghostly pale and seemed to shimmer as she hovered over a young man, her dark reddish-brown hair curling around her slender, naked shoulders. The man was no older than twenty years old and he watched her in rapt fascination as she gyrated above him, sliding her hands over his bare chest as she bent her head to kiss the smooth skin where she had touched.

She kissed a trail to his neck as he ran his freckled hands lightly over her bare back. Hovering above him, she turned her gaze to meet mine, her eyes a tranquil, calm gray.

"Help me," she whispered.

And then she plunged her teeth into the side of his neck.

He thrashed wildly and attempted to get away, but she was inhumanly strong and held him tightly to the bed until he grew limp and still while she remained fastened to his neck.

Finally, her appetite was sated and she raised her head, her gaze still locked with mine as blood streaked down her chin and dropped onto her neck.

"Help me," she repeated, speaking directly to me. And then I realized in horror that the firelight flickering against her skin was actually coming from her. Her hair wasn't auburn, it was on fire.

I screamed.

And then I was awake, grasping the bedclothes while Cadmus held me, murmuring into my ear.

"Harmonia, it's alright. You're alright. We'll find her," he soothed, stroking my back gently with large hands.

I tried to still my racing heart, to calm my rasping breath, as I studied my husband. He thought I was dreaming about our daughter again, as I had for several nights in a row. Ever since we had discovered that undoing the Fates' hold on the mortal world had also ripped our daughter from our grasp, I had dreamed of Raquel.

But not tonight.

"My love," Cadmus murmured, pulling me to his chest, "If I could take your pain and your fear away, I would do it in a moment. I hope you know that. Watching you struggle rips my heart apart."

"I feel like nothing will ever be the same," I whispered into the dark. He stilled for a moment before he answered, his voice quiet in the night.

"It won't be," he acknowledged. "But once we find our daughter, we will be better than we've ever been. Our lives will be perfect."

I closed my eyes and listened to his strong heart beat. I had known him for centuries. As my soul mate, he knew me better than anyone. He could take one look at my face and know what I was thinking, even without reading my thoughts- which he was perfectly capable of doing, as well.

I sighed and looked up to find his chocolate eyes fixed on my face.

"Cadmus, I love you. I'm sorry that I have been so distant these past few days. I have faith that we will find Raquel and bring her home. It's just that my nightmares are so vivid. When I see her screaming for me in the wastelands, it is as though I can reach out and touch her… and then she is gone. I feel so helpless. And if that weren't enough, now I'm dreaming about someone else. I don't know her, but she asked for my help." I sighed again and dropped my forehead against his warm body.

"Was this person real?" Cadmus raised a dark eyebrow. "Or is your sense of responsibility just bleeding into your dreams?"

"I don't know," I answered thinly. "It could be either one, I guess."

He pulled me closer, stroking my hair away from my forehead. His large hands were strong and comforting. He had been very patient with me these past couple of days. I knew that.

"Hush then, sweet one, and go back to sleep. I will protect you from your dreams- you need to rest. We have a long journey in front of us. You will need to be strong."

I nodded and nestled into him, willing my mind to stop churning. Cadmus was handsome, strong and he always knew my heart, but he was wrong about this. He could protect me from everything else, but he couldn't stop my dreams. Regardless, I knew he was right about needing my strength and I closed my eyes.

When I opened them again, morning light was flooding our bedchambers and Cadmus was gone. I had thankfully slept through the rest of the night without nightmares. I stretched and glanced around the room. Brilliant sunshine bounced from every surface, from the marble walls to the polished stone floors, to the massive furniture. And there was no one else here, which was strange. It was rare that I was alone.

Ever since our epic battle with the Fates and the Keres on the fields of Camelot a few days ago, someone had always made sure to be by my side… whether it was my mother, Aphrodite, my father, Ares, my sister, Ortrera or my husband. Because the Fates had managed to have the last laugh and undo my daughter's very existence after they had been dragged into the underworld by the Keres, I would readily admit that I hadn't been at my best.

A sniveling wreck would be a more accurate description.

It had taken us three days to prepare for our journey, to gather everything that the goddess of witchcraft, Hecate, had thought that we might need as we crossed the Spiritlands, the mortal world and heaven only knew where else as we hunted for the imprisoned Olympians. Without Zeus, I would never get my daughter back. He had to be found.

The mere thought of Raquel's frightened face caused my heart to start racing again and I slumped against the pillows. We had only just discovered that she was ours before she had been wrenched away. And deep in my heart, I knew she was frightened.

I could feel it with a mother's intuition. Even though I had only known myself to be a mother for a few days.

"Stop it," a quiet voice murmured.

Startled, I turned and found Hecate lingering in my doorway. Vibrant and beautiful as always, her long blonde hair tumbled to the small of her back in wavy curls. She was most certainly not what you would expect the goddess of witchcraft to look like.

"Stop torturing yourself," she insisted as she crossed to my bed. "You must. None of this is your doing. None of us, not even me, saw this coming. So get out of bed, get dressed and let us leave so that we can repair it. You will not fix anything at all from in here."

Her stern voice surprised me and my head snapped up.

"What?" she asked, her thin eyebrow raised. "Do you think I should tiptoe around you like everyone else? Yes, your daughter has been taken from you. Yes, the Olympians are hidden from us somewhere. But you are the Chosen One, Harmonia. It is time for you to start acting like it once again."

"Why are you being so mean?" I whispered as I curled my fingers deeper within my sheets, turning my face away from her. The desolation that I felt deep inside was consuming. I could hardly think past it. There was no way she could understand.

"Get up!" Hecate hissed as she threw my covers back and pulled me to my feet, ignoring my question. "This is not you, Harmonia. You are strong. You are a fighter. You are the Chosen One, for god's sake. You're the goddess of peace—summon some of that for yourself. Get up!"

I stared at her blankly, then whimpered.

"Where's Cadmus?"

She rolled her eyes and then snapped, "He's with your parents. They don't have the heart to do what I am doing now. This is called tough love. Why do you think we have taken so long to prepare for this trip? Because we have been waiting for you to regain your feisty spirit before we set off. And I was patient—you've been through a lot and you deserved a brief rest. But three days? Enough is enough! So many things hinge upon your actions, Harmonia. Your mortal mother is waiting on Calypso's island and your daughter must be found, not to mention the Olympians. Pull yourself together."

Staring into my eyes, she shook me hard. My head whipped back and I should have been angry. Or startled. Or *something.* I knew that was her intention. But I wasn't. I felt numb and when she stopped, I stood still once more with my head bowed.

"Oh, god's teeth," Hecate muttered. "I've readied a bath for you in the bathhouse. Go and bathe. We will ride at dusk."

"Why dusk?" I asked woodenly.

"Why not?" she threw over her shoulder as she walked out. "Just be ready."

I stared at her for a moment, pondering my circumstances. I had always loved a good hot bath and Zeus' bathhouse was the finest anywhere. But the mere thought of bathing was exhausting, much less actually doing it. However, the thought of suffering Hecate's wrath if she returned to find me still here spurred me into motion.

It seemed to take too much effort to summon the energy to materialize in front of the bath, so I walked instead, one numb foot after the other. I kept my eyes straight ahead, ignoring the stares from the house servants as I descended the stairs of the palace.

As I passed through the courtyard, the beauty surrounding me faded into an insignificant backdrop. The falling blue lotus blossoms, the intricate arbors dripping with jasmine, honeysuckle and climbing wisteria, the sculpted gardens that stretched as far as I could see… all of it blended together. The scents filled the air and my nose. But I didn't enjoy it as I normally did. The swirling sky above me, unique to the Spiritlands, was bright with daylight hues… pinks, whites, yellows and blues. The clouds swirled and puffed and it was a happy scene.

I should have felt brightened at the sight. But I did not. I felt empty inside.

Hecate was right. I had been through a lot lately. In the not so distant past, I had found out that for several millennia the Fates had lied to me, telling me that I was a Keeper of fate and that I was marked to carry out their plans for the mortal world. That was a lie.

For thousands of years, I had lived their lie, which typically had tragic and heartbreaking consequences for me in each life. In reality, I was the daughter of Aphrodite and Ares. And if that weren't bad enough, the Fates had somehow managed to imprison the gods.

I had already found Zeus' elusive sword, which had saved my husband Cadmus from their clutches, but when Hecate had sheathed it next to Zeus' throne, it had interfered with many things that the Fates had designed… one of them being my daughter.

Sweet little Raquel. I had only just discovered her. The Fates had hidden her from me throughout the millennia, erasing her from my memory so that I didn't even know that she was mine. Until now—and right after I had found her, she had been wrenched away. She was just…gone. It was so devastating that I didn't know if I could stand it.

"Chosen One," I muttered as I kicked a pebble on the cobblestone walk to the Bathhouse. I might be the Chosen One, meant to return the Spiritlands to Zeus, but how could I do that when I had allowed my very own daughter slip from my grasp?

Pushing open the jeweled doors, I gazed inside the massive bathhouse. It was an opulent scene straight from ancient Rome. A massive sparkling pool heated to the perfect temperature filled the majority of the room. Open hallways on either side, sculpted with flying buttresses, housed several smaller pools each fed from fountains flowing from the marble walls. White marble statues of the gods lined the backlit alcoves.

The soothing bubbling sounds filled my ears as I padded across the cut granite floor, the stone cool beneath my bare feet. It was empty but for me. Letting my soft linen sheath drop to my ankles, I stepped out of it and into the water, wading into the largest pool wearing only my bloodstone.

My bloodstone. I sighed. A gift and a curse, it had been given to me by my step-father Hephaestus in his attempt to seek revenge on my mother, Aphrodite, for betraying him with my father, Ares. Zeus had donated a bit of his own blood to Hephaestus for the cause, which had resulted in the pendant possessing powerful abilities, as well as Hephaestus' curse.

Because my memories were wiped clean in every mortal life that I had lived for the past couple of millennia, I had forgotten who I actually was and the history of my Bloodstone for a very long time. The Fates had allowed me to think that they created it instead, that it was part of their organization, the Order of the Moirae. Just another lie in an entire life filled with them.

I sighed again. The water was perfect, hot enough to steam, but not so hot that I couldn't bear it. Pulling the water back with my arms, I dropped onto my back and floated. I imagined that the water smelled like honeysuckle and instantly the flowery scent surrounded me. I stared up at the stone ceiling. It was painted with an intricate mural of Zeus and Hera presiding over a royal banquet.

Everyone in the painting was happy and joyful, laughing like carefree gods should. Aphrodite was laughing into Ares' ear while my step-father, Hephaestus, glared at them thunderously from across the room. Athena danced in lotus blossoms while Zeus wisely watched everything in front of him with a knowing smile, Hera's hand lying gently on his arm. Everyone was laughing.

Those days were gone forever unless I found them and restored them to their rightful places on Mount Olympus. With a sigh, I ducked my head underwater and kicked across the pool to the other side. There was nothing like the weight of the world on my shoulders to make me feel less than buoyant.

As I kicked off the opposing wall to return, the water began kicking up and growing choppy. I planted my feet and stared at it uncertainly. And then I froze in horror as it turned to blood. The entire pool was full of churning blood and it spattered onto my face, dripping onto my lips. Spinning in a circle, I screamed, but no one came.

And then the visions started.

Blood streamed down the marble walls of the bathhouse as I was surrounded by demons. Moaning and howling, they clawed at their monstrous faces relentlessly as they wailed. Some dragged themselves across the stone floor, their long toenails scratching as they moved. Some hobbled toward me with broken, split legs and some watched me with glittering eyes from the edges of the room.

All around me, black and gray mist drifted from the floor to the ceiling and suddenly, through it, I saw Raquel hunched over on the other side of the room. Pushing my way through the thick blood in the pool, I pulled myself over the stone ledge and sprang to my feet. Slipping across the wet floor, I raced to get to my daughter.

When I was just a few steps from her, she looked up and her jade green eyes- so like mine- were panicked and filled with terror.

"Mama, I'm scared," she whispered. "I don't like it here."

I reached out to grab her, but my fingers plunged through empty air.

She was gone.

I could practically smell her little girl smell in the air and I sank to the floor, my heart racing. I squeezed my eyes closed, trying to shut out the heart-wrenching sight of my daughter's fear. Was it real? Was someone sending me a vision or was I simply imagining it? If it was real, then it meant that Raquel still existed….somewhere. But she was clearly terrified.

"Harmonia!"

Cadmus's anxious voice echoed through the room and I opened my eyes to find him striding through the doorway with a concerned expression on his handsome face. My gaze flew around the room- everything was gone. The demons, the blood, the howling. The bath was once again filled with sparkling water. It was as if it had never happened.

I took a deep, shaky breath and sat up just as Cadmus reached me and pulled me into his arms. Clutching me to him, he kissed my forehead.

"Are you alright?" he murmured. "What is it? I sensed your fear all the way at the palace."

His dark eyes were filled with concern as he studied me and shakily, I relayed what had just happened. When I was finished, he looked around uncertainly at the sparkling calm waters and soothing fountains.

"How frightening for you," he answered softly.

"It happened," I insisted. "I'm not crazy, Cadmus."

"Of course you're not," he soothed, stroking my back. "But you have had a lot of strain of late. And that takes its toll on a person."

I should have felt comforted by him, but suddenly I just felt alone. He didn't believe me. My shoulders slumped and I sagged against him. He lifted my chin with a finger.

"Harmonia, I love you more than life. I do. And we'll get through this. Do you believe me?"

Bending his head, he kissed me, gently at first and then when I responded, he grew more passionate and fiery. Groaning, he pulled me to him and ran his hands over my naked back, trailing down to my hips.

"I've missed you, wife," he murmured against my lips. "Come back to me. Please."

The desperation in his voice struck a chord deep within me and ignited a spark. I pushed him backward onto the floor and dropped onto his chest, kissing him with all of the pent-up emotion that I had been holding inside. His dark beauty caused my heart to flutter as he grinned a brilliant white smile before he raised his head to kiss a frantic trail on my neck. The water in the pools began churning from our energy and I closed my eyes, allowing him to soothe me in the best way a husband could.

Twenty minutes later, we lay spent on the cool marble.

My cheeks were flushed and I was tired, but for the first time in three days, I felt alive. And more like myself. As I propped myself up on one arm to tell Cadmus that very thing, a flash of color caught my eye.

Glancing at the back wall, I froze. Words written in blood dripped down the stone.

*Oracle of the Dead.*

# Chapter Two

Within minutes, my parents and Hecate joined us in the bathhouse and we examined the bloody words on the wall.

"Who wrote this?" Ares demanded of Hecate. She stared back at him with raised eyebrows.

"War god, why do you always assume that I am all-knowing simply because I am the goddess of witchcraft?"

He ignored the question.

"Do you know who wrote these words?"he demanded again impatiently.

She dropped her gaze and sighed. "No."

"But we know where to find this oracle," Aphrodite interrupted grimly.

"We do?" I asked in surprise. "Where?"

"She can be summoned in the Necramanteion. It's a temple ruins on the banks of the Acheron river in Greece. I know the place."

"Well, why do we wait?" I looked at them. "Let's move." I began walking toward the door when Hecate stepped forward and grabbed my arm.

"It isn't that easy, Chosen One," she muttered. "Or that smart."

"Why?" I stared at her.

"It isn't easy because the Oracle must be paid and the price is different for every person who seeks her. And it isn't smart because we have no idea who left us this message."

"You think someone attempts to lead us into a trap?"

I could practically see the bristling hairs on Cadmus' neck as he spoke. His warrior's senses were on full alert, I could tell.

"That's the problem, Cadmus," she answered. "We do not know."

"Well, then, let us find out," I muttered impatiently. "We should go now."

Hecate shook her head gently. "As I said, it is not that easy. There are preparations to be made before we can approach the Oracle."

"Preparations?" I was hesitant now. My mother stepped forward, her lovely face a blank mask. Because of her expression, I instantly knew that she was trying to hide something from me and that put me on guard. But before I could ask anything, she spoke.

"Someone seeks the Oracle of the Dead in order to speak to those who have crossed over into death. I have no idea why we would need her counsel."

I looked at the people surrounding me and no one was meeting my gaze.

"You think it's about Raquel," I whispered. "You think she is dead, don't you? I saw her just a moment ago. She was alive and she was afraid."

Cadmus pulled me to him stoically.

"Harmonia, whatever it is about, we will face it together. We will go, we will listen to the Oracle and then we will find our daughter."

I gazed into his chocolate brown eyes for just a moment, blocking out everyone else in the room. His dark hair curled slightly around the nape of his neck, his chiseled jaw strong and clenched as he appraised me. He and everyone else here thought that I was fragile, that I might break at any moment. That much was apparent. And yesterday, this morning, even an hour ago, that might have been the case. But for whatever unexplainable reason, I was stronger now.

"I'm fine," I told him softly as I reached up to kiss him gently on the lips. "I feel strong. I'm ready to go. I'm sorry that I've been weak the past couple of days. But I can face whatever we need to now. I promise you."

My mother rushed to me, sweeping me into her slender arms, enclosing me into a vise-like embrace. She looked deceptively fragile and small- but in reality, she was strong enough to lift a stack of cars. She smelled like lavender and sweetpeas.

"You have no idea how happy that makes me," she gushed into my neck as she hugged me close. "I've been so worried. We didn't know what to do for you- you weren't yourself and---"

"Aphrodite, let her breathe," Ares said gruffly as he pulled her away. Looking at me, he said, "It's good to have you back, daughter."

I nodded, holding Cadmus' strong arm close.

"What do we need to do to prepare for the Oracle?" I asked, intent on changing the subject as I blinked back hot tears.

"It's not easy," Hecate warned. "The Oracle insists that those who seek her come with a clear mind and an unpolluted heart. Because of that, she will not come unless you fast in solitude for two days and nights on the hills outside of her ruins."

"Alone?" I asked.

"Alone," Hecate nodded. "We can all go at once, of course. But we will each need to stay on separate spots on the hillside. It's a fairly desolate place. We will not be bothered."

"Well then," I swallowed hard. "Let us go. Now. There is no reason to wait."

Ares laughed in satisfaction, throwing his dark head back.

"My daughter has truly returned to us. What spirit! We will need to gather your sister and her warriors, of course."

I nodded. "Of course. Ortrera would be agitated if we left her behind."

"That's putting it mildly," Hecate muttered and I had to smile.

My half-sister, Ortrera, was a queen of the Amazons. She was as hard as nails. She was a six feet tall lithe wall of muscle. Her face was beautiful in a very fierce way and she was deeply loyal to her family. She had helped us in more ways than one over the years.

And she was as tough as anyone I had ever seen. No one in their right mind should mess with her. Ever.

"Alright," my mother said briskly. "Ares, summon the Amazons. Harmonia, you and Cadmus can accompany me back to the palace. Hecate… you can do whatever it is that witches do."

Hecate glowered at her. "I'll accompany you also, thanks."

"Suit yourself," my mother sniffed, turning to glide toward the door.

I offered a small smile to Hecate behind my mother's back. Hecate had proven to be a good friend throughout the last few months. Aphrodite did truly like the witch, but due to my mother's dramatic nature, she was sometimes a bit jealous.

As we emerged onto the pristine walkway that led to the palace, the sun shone on my shoulders and this time, I did allow it to brighten my mood. Just having a plan and a place to begin made me feel better- like we would manage to once again be successful. Only this time, it had to be a complete success. Failure in any way simply wasn't an option.

As Cadmus and I entered our bedchambers, I turned to him.

"How does one prepare for a solitary fast on an abandoned hillside?"

He pulled me into his arms, gently supporting my weight as he lowered us onto the softness of our bed.

"By feasting on everything that we will miss, of course."

He laughed and I couldn't help but laugh with him. I laid my head against his chest and felt it rumble with his laughter and I closed my eyes. This man was everything- my entire world. No matter what would come, we would face it together as we always had. We would be okay. I nestled into his hard body and inhaled his familiar, woodsy scent.

I woke up screaming.

I hadn't planned on falling asleep, but my emotional state had left me drained. But the pain… the pain is what awakened me. The bird shaped birthmark on my wrist was on fire.

Literally.

I sat straight up on the bed, clutching my arm to my chest as I tried to block out the overwhelming pain. It hurt so much that the light in the room blended together and I couldn't see straight. Cadmus frantically turned my arm over to examine it and we both gasped. My birth mark had grown to encompass the entire width of my wrist and had stretched to become three inches long. Its outline was literally burning and the air crackled with the sound of sizzling flesh.

The mark had also changed. It was now a clear outline of the Phoenix. It looked more like a flaming tattoo than a birthmark. After a moment, the burning embers died, leaving a blackened phoenix imprint.

My gaze met that of my husband and we stared at each other for a moment.

"What does this mean?" I whispered.

"I do not know," he admitted. "Perhaps Hecate will know something."

I nodded, but a feeling of dread curled around my stomach with icy fingers. This couldn't mean anything good.

"Cadmus..." my voice trailed off uncertainly. I cleared it impatiently. "I have never actually seen the prophecy, have you?"

He shook his head grimly, his chocolate eyes frozen on my face. "No."

"I think it's time that I read it for myself, don't you?"

He grasped my hand, rubbing a circle on my thumb.

"Alright. But Harmonia, I am concerned. I do not wish for you to become upset by anything that we see. A prophecy does not mean that something will certainly come to pass. We still have free will. And that means... that means that we can change anything that we put our minds to."

I smiled gently at him, reaching out to stroke his handsome face. He leaned into my hand, taking a deep breath.

"I know," I replied softly. "But I have to see it. I've heard bits and pieces but have never actually read it. I have only seen the page from the book in Hecate's cave. I don't even know whose prophecy it is. I feel like I will be stronger and can understand it more if I just read it myself."

He sighed long and loud, but extended his hand. "Then let us go," he suggested. "We do not have much time. Let us find it."

I took his hand and allowed him to pull me from the bed. He kept a tight grip on my hand as we made our way to the main floor of the palace. The marble floors sparkled in the light pouring in from the windows and I found my mother sitting in a cushioned seat by the back terrace.

"Harmonia, you're awake!" she exclaimed, rising to meet us. "I'm glad you were able to rest. We're making preparations for the trip. Your father is with your sister and Hecate is in her cave. We are meeting back here at dusk. Are you ready?"

I nodded. "I will be, mother. But first there are just two things I need to do."

"There are?" She was puzzled.

"Yes," I confirmed. "I need to see my mortal mother—to know that she is alright before we depart and I need to read the prophecy for myself. I wish to see what it says… in its entirety."

Her face instantly turned into an unreadable mask and I tensed.

"Mother," I began uncertainly. "I feel as though you are hiding something from me. And I wish to know what it is."

Sunlight bathed my mother in backlit loveliness as I waited for a response. I didn't receive one.

"Mother," I repeated. "I need to know. Where can I find it?"

"Harmonia," she sighed. "There is no reason for you to read it. We've told you what you need to know and time is of the essence now. I don't think it's—"

I cut her off.

"Mother, where is it?"

Her silver gaze met mine for an extended moment and hers finally wavered.

"Very well," she replied. "It is in the libraries. But I really wish you wouldn't."

"Your concern has been noted," I answered glibly. "But I need to do this."

Her shoulders slumped and she looked to Cadmus.

"Cadmus..."

"She feels strongly about this, Aphrodite," he replied firmly. "It is not for us to keep it from her."

"Fine," she muttered. "But I see no reason to upset yourself at this juncture." She turned her back on us and stared once again out the windows. The fact that she felt this strongly made me uneasy and I looked up at Cadmus.

"Are you ready?"I murmured.

He nodded and grasped my elbow, leading me from the great room and down the hall to Zeus' massive libraries. We waited outside of the agate doors, hesitating just a moment while I gathered my thoughts.

I nodded and Cadmus pushed the doors open.

Late afternoon sunlight streamed in through the glass ceiling. It was as quiet as a tomb, the air still and silent. The room was a large as a gymnasium and it was filled with shelves from floor to ceiling. Leather bound books and pyramid-shaped stacks of rolled parchments filled the shelves. Any little noise that we made echoed loudly throughout the open corridors.

An enormous falcon, a personal pet of Zeus himself, sat on a perch directly inside the door. He had gold bands wrapped around his thick scaly legs. He swiveled his head to stare at me with onyx eyes. As his gaze met mine, he dropped his head in deference.

"I've been waiting for you," he croaked hoarsely. "Show me your mark."

I silently approached him and turned my wrist over. The phoenix imprint was still tender, a bright, angry crimson rimmed in charred black.

"Ah, so it begins," the bird mused. "You may enter."

I glanced at Cadmus uncertainly, but stepped forward into the massive library. There were too many books. I had no idea where to start.

"Where should we begin?" I asked Cadmus.

"Follow your heart," the bird interjected knowingly. "You are tied to everything, Harmonia. You must simply listen."

Cadmus raised his eyebrow at the bird questioningly, but I closed my eyes.

My heart thudded in my chest rhythmically, like a drum. I focused on it and allowed myself to feel every reverberation throughout my body. I could feel the pulse in my feet, the blood rushing through my veins, my bloodstone lying coolly on my chest. My heart beat against it.

And then I felt a pull. Willingly, I opened up my mind and allowed the pull to move me. I walked forward and Cadmus stayed at my side. I wound my way through the rows of books and stood in front of a shelf in the back corner where the light almost didn't reach.

I knew I was in the right spot. I knew it with unexplainable certainty.

Suddenly, a rolled parchment fell from the top shelf and landed at my feet. Before I could even move, Cadmus bent and picked it up, untying the velvet string and unrolling the parchment.

I watched his jaw tighten as he read the words inscribed on the page. His beautiful dark eyes hardened and I felt the stirrings of dread.

"What is it?" I whispered hesitantly. He shook his head.

"It's nothing. This is just a silly premonition by someone we don't even know…"

The falcon fluttered from the top of a nearby bookcase and landed in front of us.

"The Oracle of the Dead brought us this prophecy," he told us. "She has never been wrong, not even once."

"The Oracle prophesied this?" I asked tremulously.

The bird nodded once, his black eyes shining in the light. I gulped and held my hand out to Cadmus. He didn't move.

"Cadmus," I prompted. He sighed and handed it to me.

***The Prophecy of The Chosen One***

*She who will save Olympus and all that we know.*

*Treacherous snakes will tremble beneath her fingers and the crown shall be restored.*

*Despite great sadness and loss, she will prevail,*
*As she alone holds the noblest and purest of hearts.*
*The Chosen One will save everyone but perhaps herself.*

*At what cost will order be restored?*
*Will she perish in the flames of the Phoenix,*
*Never to rise to the land of the living once more?*

*Time will tell.*

My breath caught in my throat as I read and Cadmus wrapped his arms around me, pressing his forehead to mine.

"It means nothing," he insisted. "We choose our destiny, remember, Harmonia? The Fates are imprisoned in the Underworld. We choose our own fates now. I will never allow anything to happen to you. Do you understand?"

I nodded to placate him, but my heart was racing.

"Time will tell," I murmured.

"No," Cadmus said harshly. "I can tell you right now. This is not right. We will be victorious, but you will be fine. You have faced death already in Camelot. Remember? Perhaps that is what this is referring to. You came back from that. You are fine."

I had a feeling that Camelot was not what this prophecy referred to, but I didn't say it. Instead, I folded into Cadmus' side and allowed him to hold me for just a moment.

I closed my eyes and inhaled his strength, his scent, even his heart beat. I picked up his hand and held it to my heart.

"My love?"The anxiety in his voice pulled at my heart strings and I opened my eyes.

"I'm fine," I assured him. "I only need to see my mortal mother- and then I will be ready."

"Harmonia, we should talk about this prophecy further. I don't think—"

I cut him off.

"Cadmus, I'm fine. There is no use in talking about it. Whatever happens will happen. It is what it is. I will not worry about it now- there are too many other things to be concerned with."

I nodded curtly at the falcon and strode across the room for the door. As I entered the hall, I was met by Hecate.

"You saw?" she raised her eyebrow.

"Yes," I confirmed.

"You're fine?"

"Yes."

"Good. I know you would like to see your mother before we depart. Come with me."

Without questioning her or how she knew that that was exactly what I had been intent on, Cadmus and I followed her to the courtyard to a small pond in the center. Koi swam leisurely in circles in the clear, cool water. Hecate waved her hand and they froze. The water rippled only once and then Calypso's island appeared on the surface.

My mortal mother, Allison Lockhart, was walking on a pristine beach with Calypso. She was healthy and well, her dark hair blowing in the sea breeze as she laughed at something that Calypso said.

The island was clearly being kind to her. Her skin was sun-kissed, her cheeks pleasantly flushed. I knew that she didn't even remember who she was at this point. Calypso's Island was enchanted and it stole the consciousness of anyone who entered. It was as if a strange fog descended onto one's mind there.

My stomach tightened as I watched and I suddenly desperately missed my mother. I still had to decide what to do with that situation. My mother had no idea who I truly was. When I returned from this quest, I would have to deal with that. If I stayed here in Olympus, I would miss her so much. But the thought of returning to the mortal world simply didn't seem feasible anymore. I no longer felt like Macy Lockhart in the slightest bit. I had reclaimed my true goddess identity and I didn't see any way that I could realistically go back.

"We'll think on that later, love," Cadmus murmured as he read my mind. I nodded. He was right. There was no reason to focus on it now.

I turned to Hecate.

"Thank you."

She waved her hand at the small pool and it returned to normal. The koi circled it once again, swimming lazy circles.

"We should go," she prodded me. "We've delayed long enough. There is much to be done."

I nodded and took Cadmus' arm as we returned to the palace. Hecate's filmy white cloak fluttered in the breeze as we walked and I stared at it absently, trying to mentally prepare myself for what was to come. Whatever it was, it was not going to be pleasant.

Ares, Ortrera and her warriors and my mother were all congregated in the great room of the palace when we arrived. Ares was holding Zeus' sword, turning it over and over as he spoke with Ortrera. When we walked in, he plunged it into a sheath at his side before crossing to me.

"You're fine?" he demanded. It was more of a dictate than a question. I nodded.

"I'm fine."

"You take after me," he noted, his handsome face clearly reflecting his pride. My mother scowled.

"Perhaps in her bull-headedness," Aphrodite acknowledged.

I grabbed her hand.

"Are you ready?"

"Not really," she admitted, her beautiful face troubled. "But it is time."

Hecate stepped forward.

"Yes, it is time. What we do now will not be easy, that we know," she began.

The Amazons murmured their agreement.

"But it is necessary and we will do it. We are strong and we will prevail. Harmonia, you have seen the prophecy. Let us prove the undesirable parts wrong. You will be fine and we will make sure that you return safely here... no matter where this journey takes us. Let us finish this."

We all joined hands and stood in a circle as Hecate began to chant. I felt the familiar weakening of my limbs as we faded out of the Spiritlands and reappeared on a barren hillside in the mortal world.

It was approaching nightfall and there was no civilization as far as I could see. Cadmus clenched my hand tighter. The grass beneath our feet was thick and lush with scattered stones and boulders throughout the hills. There were no trees, just rolling hills and waving grass all along the banks of a wide river.

The Acheron river. It was said that it continued from the mortal world into the depths of the Underworld. It was known as the river of pain. I gulped and took a deep breath, glancing up the hill.

The temple ruins stood at the top on the edge of the banks. They were made from crumbling stone and seemed as much a part of the landscape as the natural rocks and grass.

"We cannot approach yet," Hecate pointed out as she followed my gaze. "First, we must spend two days fasting here, clearing our minds and purifying our hearts."

She held out her hands. In each one, she held dried herbs.

"To help clear your mind," she answered my unspoken question. We all took a dried leaf and dutifully chewed it up. I felt no different.

"We must separate," Hecate instructed. "We should each find a different location on this hill and spend the next two days reflecting on ourselves and our plight. And then, hopefully, we will be in the right frame of mind to summon the Oracle."

We all nodded and separated into different directions. Cadmus grabbed my elbow and drew me in to him.

"You will be fine," he assured me. I stared into his eyes.

"I know," I answered. "I am not concerned- you are."

He smiled. "That's true," he admitted. "I am concerned about you. That is my job as your husband."

"Hmm," I pondered with a smile. "I seem to recall that I saved your hide in the not so distant past. Perhaps I will be saving it again- I am the Chosen One, after all."

He threw his head back and laughed. "You *are* a cheeky one," he chuckled. "It's one of the reasons that I love you."

"I'll be fine," I told him seriously. "We all will. Let's just get this over with."

He pulled me closer and kissed me soundly. I melted into his strong body for a scant moment before pulling back.

"I'll see you soon," I promised.

"Not soon enough," he mumbled as he disappeared into the dark. I watched the outline of his tall shape for as long as I could until he was completely gone before I turned and studied my surroundings.

There was simply nothing here.

The rushing sound of the river drew me to it and I decided to choose a spot close to the water. There was a little horse-shoe shaped inlet filled with sand and rock and I dropped onto it from the banks, allowing my bare feet to sink into the cool sand.

It was still and peaceful here and I lifted my face to the night breeze. It smelled of damp earth and river water. I tossed my pack onto a nearby rock before I conjured a small bonfire. Curling up next to it, leaning against a boulder, I allowed myself to become mesmerized by the flames. Ever since I had learned that I controlled the Phoenix, fire had become such a fascination. It was almost like I was drawn to it. Unbidden, the words of the prophecy returned to me.

*Will she perish in the flames of the Phoenix,*
*Never to rise to the land of the living once more?*

What in the world did that mean? I shook my head, trying to shake the troublesome thoughts. I was supposed to be clearing my mind, not muddling them up with worries. So once again, I stared into the flames.

I startled awake. I had fallen asleep without even knowing it. Somewhere in the distance, I heard an owl hooting into the night. And then there was no other sound but for the rush of the river. My campfire had gone out, so I conjured it again. Soon, orange flame lit the night and warmed my skin.

I was also surprised to find my vision just a little blurred. Since assuming my true goddess identity once again, I had become accustomed to the startling clarity that came with that. Normally, my vision was perfect, my mind was sharp and my body was agile and strong. But right now, it almost felt as though I had had too much to drink.

I staggered to my feet and leaned against the river bank. The prickly grass poked me in the back, but it didn't matter. I scarcely felt it. The rumble of the river had turned into a vague hum in the back of my consciousness as the inky blackness of night enveloped me.

*Help me.*

The whisper hissed from the shadows and I spun, clumsily losing my balance and tripping in the wet sand. I righted myself and shoved the hair out of my face with shaking fingers.

*Help me.*

I felt warm breath graze my ear and I spun again.

The young woman from my dream stood in the moonlight directly to my right. She was beautiful in a fragile, ethereal way. Her skin was pale, her hair dark, her eyes a clear gray. But her face… her face is what grasped my attention and held it. It was delicate and lovely, but the expression was so tortured that it wrenched at my heart. What was causing her so much pain?

"Who are you?" I whispered. She stepped toward me with one slender hand outstretched.

"Save me," she murmured. "Please."

"Who are you?" I cried again. She shook her head sadly and stepped from the bank into the river. Wading away from me, she looked over her shoulder one time before she faded into the night.

I was shaken and I slipped to the ground in a crouch as I tried to catch my breath. Who the heck was she? Why was she asking for my help?

"Mama?"

A small, thin voice rose from the darkness, interrupting my frantic thoughts and causing the breath to catch in my throat.

"Raquel," I answered in a whisper.

"Mama, I don't like it here."

My eyes flew to the horizon and I found her small body hunched over. She was scratching at the wet sand with a stick, her hair a dark curtain hiding her face. I scrambled to my feet and rushed toward her, but when I was three steps away, she lifted her sweet little face to me.

"Don't come here, mama. You won't like it, either."

And she was gone. I stepped closer to where she had been and stopped short as I saw the word that she had etched out in the sand.

*HELL.*

But before I could process that, blood seemed to pour from the sky, raining onto me and coloring the river red. It soaked my clothes and washed away my daughter's writing. I shook my head in horror and whirled around, trying to see in every direction at once.

"It's not real," I whispered. "It's not."

As if in contradiction, a trickle of blood ran across my foot, streaming down the wet sand until it dumped into the river.

"It's not real," I insisted. I knew I was talking to myself, that regardless of my visions, no one else was here with me. Yet still, the hair on the back of my neck remained raised and the goose bumps still clung to my arms. I blinked my eyes hard and when I re-opened them, the blood was gone. Why had all of my visions of late involved so much blood? I could only imagine that it had some significance, but what?

As I pondered that, a long, thick green speckled snake slithered out of the river and coiled itself in front of me. I quickly stepped back, but before I could scream, two more had joined it, and then three more and then five. Snakes were coming from everywhere…crawling from the river and dropping from the trees.

I could hear the smooth rustle of their bellies against the wet ground as they congregated around me. Every reptilian head was pointed toward me, each slitted eye fixated on me.

The snake in front raised its head and hissed.

"Liessss."

The rest of them raised their heads in unison, swaying in the breeze as they all hissed.

"Liesssss."

It seemed to echo in the night, their hissing lisps resounding in my head as I backed away from them and tried to scramble to safety. In my haste, I tripped on a fallen branch and sprawled halfway into the murky water before dragging myself back out and looking over my shoulder.

The snakes were gone.

Breathing raggedly, I propped myself against the bank of the Acheron and crossed my legs in front of me. I happened to notice that my foot was blood-spattered…evidence that my visions had truly happened. I wasn't crazy. I wasn't sure if that was a relief or not. I might actually prefer to be crazy.

I leaned my head back against the spindly river grass and closed my eyes.

When I opened them again, it was daylight and I wasn't alone.

A large owl, probably the one I had heard in the night, was standing a few feet away from me, watching me as I slept with sharp amber eyes. I shook the sleep from my eyes and studied it.

From all appearances, it seemed to be a normal owl. But I knew from the rapt attention it was paying me that it was anything but normal.

"What do you want?" I asked impatiently. I had had it with avian messengers.

It blinked its round eyes at me, but remained silent.

"Well?" I demanded. "What do you want?"

It suddenly shrieked and unfurled its wings, startling me.

And then I was falling. And falling. And falling.

I hit the ground in a sprawl and looked around in confusion. Blackness was everywhere. People were crying and moaning and crawling along the ransacked ground. It was a scene that could have been taken from a horrifying apocalyptic movie. And then there was the blood.

A river of blood ran in the middle of the cracked, dry ground. The rusty smell filled my nostrils and I cringed as I climbed to my feet.

A hollow-eyed, hunched over man stood in front of me as he grinned wickedly with yellowed teeth.

"You are betrayed," he crooned eerily. "You will be betrayed… You have been betrayed…. You are betrayed." He was singing in an evil voice as he crept away from me and I could hear him even as he disappeared from my sight. "Betrayed."

Icy hands from the bodies crawling along the ground gripped at my ankles and I swatted them away.

And then I was standing back by the Acheron in the same spot where I had been.

I was upright, on my feet, in broad daylight. I looked around in disorientation. I had never left. I had been here all along- but now the owl was gone. What the hell was happening to me?

Dizziness consumed me and I closed my eyes. It was just too much. Even with my eyes closed, the world was spinning and I lost my hold on reality. I fell onto the wet sand and my last conscious thought was of a hissing whisper.

"Betrayed."

# Chapter Three

"Harmonia."

I could hear someone through a dark pool, calling my name. I moved away, curling up on the ground. I didn't want any part of even one more crazy vision.

"Harmonia," the voice was clear and melodic. And vaguely familiar.

I reluctantly opened my eyes to find a white blur in front of me amidst a sea of blurred objects. I blinked hard and tried again. Still blurry.

I stubbornly held my eyes open and a woman slowly came into focus.

Hecate.

I could've cried from relief. The rest of the group quickly came into focus behind her. Cadmus looked only slightly worse for the wear as he swept in and pulled me into his arms.

"Are you alright?" he asked anxiously, quickly giving me the once over. I nodded, although when I did, the world started spinning again and I closed my eyes.

"The dizziness will pass," Hecate said knowingly. "But now our minds and hearts are unpolluted. We are free to seek the Oracle. Attempt to keep a clear mind- do not think on anything that troubles you."

That was more difficult than it sounded. I instantly wanted to ponder my disturbing visions, so I had to fight to keep them at bay. But I could think on them later. For now, I grasped Cadmus' arm tightly.

"Are you well?" I asked quietly, reaching up to smooth his dark hair into place.

"I am much better now, my love," he smiled.

"Have we truly been here for two entire days? I think I've slept most of the time." I looked around in bewilderment. Aphrodite looked as disheveled as I felt. She nodded in agreement.

"I feel the same," she admitted, smoothing out the pleats in her short, belted skirt. "This has not been a pleasant experience, Hecate."

"I never said that it would be," Hecate replied grimly. "And I fear it will not get any better. Come now, let us go."

I took a few faltering steps, but my legs felt like rubber and I paused.

"Hecate, what did you give us? I feel as weak as a newborn baby."

She appraised me for a moment thoughtfully before answering.

"The herbs would not have left you so bereft, Chosen One. I believe it has been the strength of your visions that has drained you. You will regain your strength soon- you are strong."

I nodded, but still didn't feel confident enough to take another step.

Cadmus bent and slipped his arms under my knees, lifting me to his chest just like an infant.

"Rest, my love," he instructed as he climbed the steep hillside with me in his arms.

"This isn't necessary," I protested. But even as I spoke, I rested my head against his hard chest. I knew Hecate was right. Worse things were to come. I might as well rest in the comfort of my husband's arms while I could.

We quickly reached the top of the hill and we stood in a quiet group outside of the ruins. It was completely silent and still and I felt the hair lift on the back of my neck. Cadmus gently set me down and I stood uncertainly next to him.

"What do we do now?" I asked.

"We summon her," Hecate answered simply. Walking purposefully in front of us, she bypassed the ruins and stood behind it, directly in front of a large urn-like vessel. It was ancient, that much was apparent. I had the feeling it had survived thousands of years in this spot.

"We must offer her something of relevance," Hecate said without turning around. "Harmonia, come here."

Cadmus released my arm and I stepped forward hesitantly. The tone of Hecate's voice unnerved me. It was cold and perfunctory.

"Harmonia, you must know that your blood is significant. Have your visions attested to that?" Hecate asked, her blue eyes glittering.

"There has been quite a lot of blood in my visions, yes," I confirmed. "But not necessarily mine. Just... blood."

Hecate smiled a haunting smile, her face so wise and knowing. I was reminded once again that she was very, very old, older even than Zeus himself. It was easy to sometimes forget that because she seemed so young and beautiful. But when she spoke, those around her should certainly listen. Her magic was powerful, her wisdom revered. She watched me now, her vibrant blue eyes shimmering.

"Ah, young one. Blood is relevant no matter what the situation is. It is who we are. There is much to be learned from someone's blood. Their heart, their identity, their purpose. Particularly in matters pertaining to the gods because there is always such deceit. Blood can reveal the truth. But in your case, it will always be a key."

She turned to look at me, her face calm and impassive.

"Come forward, Harmonia."

She extended her hand and I took it, stepping forward until I stood directly in front of the peeling, clay urn. Hecate flipped up the hem of her skirt and pulled a dagger from the belt around her thigh. I stiffened as she turned my arm over.

Quickly, she sliced a small cut in the heart of my phoenix mark and held it over the mouth of a silver cup. My blood dripped into the cup and I tried not to flinch as I stood still and watched it. After what seemed like forever, she dropped my arm. Moving forward, she set the silver goblet into the urn and stepped back.

"Close your eyes," Hecate instructed us without turning around.

Trustingly, we all did as she asked, listening to her guttural, incoherent chants.

Minutes passed and I ached to open my eyes, but I withstood the temptation. After another minute more, however, a cold chill descended upon me and goose bumps formed on my arms. Something had shifted. The air was cold and heavy, and a palpable foreboding hung all around me in the air.

"I am here," a chilling voice announced quietly. "Why have you summoned me?"

I opened my eyes and almost gasped.

The Oracle was a frightening sight. She was as pale as a ghost, perched on a gnarled, tall stool that hadn't been there just a scant moment ago. She seemed to almost float. She was naked, but for a dark, crimson hooded cloak. Her face was barely visible from beneath the hood. The cloak was wrapped loosely around her, so loosely that her naked body, riddled with blue scrawling veins, was apparent.

As she hunched over, she held the goblet of my blood in her hands and it was clear that she had drunk from it. My blood streaked down her chin. She slowly lifted the cup again and took another long sip. As she did, she moaned a long shaking sigh.

"I saw visions of you long ago," she whispered. "So long ago. And now you are here before me. You are ready to fulfill the prophecy, are you not?"

Her whispers were quiet, but they held so much weight. They cut the air like a scalpel and we hung on every word.

I nodded.

She slowly turned her face to meet my gaze and once again, I wanted to gasp but did not. Her eyes were made from blood. They were not bleeding as the Keres did, hers were different. They had no pupil or iris or white. They *were* blood. My stomach turned queasy and I gripped my hands together tightly.

"Will you do what you must?" she queried. "No matter the personal cost, will you pay it?"

I paused. What would be asked of me? What did I have to give? But in that moment, a vision of my daughter's young, innocent face formed in my mind and I knew that I would give anything. It did not matter what was asked of me, if I had it to give, I would.

I nodded.

"Yes," I whispered.

"No matter the cost?" she persisted.

"No matter the cost," I confirmed softly. My knees felt weak, but I did not flinch or move. I prayed that she did not sense my fear.

"You will face challenges that seem insurmountable," she stated calmly. "You must focus on your purpose and on your strength and you will persevere. There will be times when you question even each other. Focus on the love that you have and you will overcome."

I chanced a sidelong glance at everyone else. They were watching the Oracle in rapt fascination.

"Harmonia."

She drew my attention back to her in a raspy whisper.

"You may have one question answered, but only one. Choose wisely."

My mind instantly whirled. What should I ask? Did I want to know if I lived or died? What obstacles would we face? No. I knew without question what I wanted to ask and I didn't hesitate.

"Where is my daughter?"

She cocked her head and studied me.

"She is where you must go," she answered cryptically. "When you reach her, you will find all that you seek."

"But where is that?" I asked tremulously.

"You will find her in the Underworld." The Oracle nodded slowly. And I thought back to the word Raquel had scratched into the sand. HELL. I gulped hard.

"And everyone else? They are in the Underworld also?"

"I am only able to answer one question," the Oracle replied, her voice an eerie creak. "Only one. Have faith, Chosen One, and you will prevail."

She began fading until only her eyes were visible, and then they disappeared as well.

"I will prevail," I repeated. "But will I survive it?"

I turned and faced my parents, my husband, my sister and her warriors. They didn't have an answer for me, but my husband's jaw was clenched.

"Of course you will survive it," he insisted. "I will make sure of it."

I smiled gently at him. "We should go. Our daughter is waiting."

I turned to Hecate. "How do we get there?"

She motioned to the old ruins. "This temple is an entrance to the Underworld. Follow me."

"How convenient," I muttered. But I stood aside and allowed her to walk past me into the ruins.

Cadmus clasped his hand around mine and we followed her silently, while my parents followed us and Ortrera and her warriors followed them. We were a silent procession as we made our way to the tunnel. It wasn't long before we stood in front of it.

The mouth of the old tunnel yawned black and wide and there was a chilling air of foreboding surrounding it. Even if I hadn't known what it was, I would have sensed the importance that it contained.

I looked to Hecate.

"Well?"

"Well, what?" she raised an eyebrow. "Enter."

I eyed the hall. The blackness was consuming and the chill emanating from it sent goose-bumps rippling over my body.

"It's that simple?" I whispered.

The corners of her mouth twitched. "Entering is the easy part," she answered. "Enter with a pure heart and a clear purpose and the tunnel will give way."

I squeezed Cadmus' hand for strength and took a faltering step and then another. I could smell the damp and the mold as we descended into the passageway. And then, just as Hecate said, the hall extended. And then extended more with every step that we took. I couldn't see anything as I felt my way along. It was utterly dark. I heard the rest of the group following closely behind me and I took comfort in that. We certainly were not alone.

Before I had gone twenty more paces, I recognized the trickling sound of water. It grew into a roar. And then we spilled out from the narrow passage into a large torch-lit cavern filled with a river. The river Styx. I knew it even without asking Hecate.

The river Styx was the boundary between the mortal world and the Underworld. From here on out, nothing would be the same. There would be a new set of rules. I looked to Hecate. She traveled between these worlds frequently. She knew the rules better than anyone.

"We wait," she answered my unspoken question. "The ferryman will be along soon."

I couldn't contain my nerves as I glanced around at my companions. We were preparing to go where the living didn't usually tread.

My father stood stoically with my mother, his arm draped casually over her shoulders. I shouldn't have been surprised. Very few things in life unnerved him. My mother actually seemed calm, which was unusual. Most things in life unnerved her. As I would have expected, Ortrera and her warriors stood impassively at attention. They prided themselves on never showing emotion.

I gazed up at my husband and found him watching me, his dark eyes pensive.

"Are you alright?" he murmured, lightly rubbing my shoulders. I nodded wordlessly. I had to be, didn't I? There was no choice for me. This was the way it must be.

The sound of oars pushing through water distracted me and I craned my neck. The ferryman glided to a stop in front of us. His boat was ancient. The wood creaked with the movement of the water and moss grew along its bottom. The boatman himself stood facing us, a questioning look on his sharp, angular face. Given how long he had been at this job, I expected him to be very old. But he was not. He was solidly middle-aged, although his face was weathered.

"What is the meaning of this?" he demanded. "Hecate! This is highly unorthodox."

Hecate stepped forward to face him.

"Charon," she began soothingly. "I realize it is unusual, but we have very important business here, old friend. It is of utmost importance that you take us to the gates. The entire world could very well hinge upon it."

He spat into the muddy water, his hawk-like face curled into a scowl.

"What care have I regarding the world?" he demanded. "*This* is my world- and it has been for thousands of years. I care not what happens to mortals before they come to me."

"It is not only mortals of which I speak," Hecate pointed out softly. "It is everyone, gods and mortals alike. Charon, please. I would not normally ask such a thing. But this is crucial."

He cocked his head and examined her. "I'll admit, it is not like you to beg," he finally acknowledged. "You are much too proud. Fine. Pay the fare and I will take you."

She smiled a beatific smile. "Thank you, Charon." She dug into her cloak and pulled out a handful of drachmas. "I am indebted to you."

She turned and offered me her hand. "Come, Harmonia." I stepped forward and she helped me into the rocking boat, followed quickly by everyone else.

Charon barely waited for the last Amazon warrior to step into the boat before he pushed away from shore and quickly sailed down the river towards the Underworld. I clenched the side of the boat tightly as we moved and glancing down, I saw that we weren't actually sitting in the water at all. The ferry was hovering just above the river.

We moved from the confines of the dark passage into a vast expanse of space where the blackness of night enveloped us and the river flowed downward through midair. I peered over the side of the boat and saw that there was nothing below us as far as I could see. If I fell from the ferry, it looked as though I would fall forever. I clenched the side tighter.

Cadmus leaned forward. "It will be fine, wife."

I raised an eyebrow. "And how do you know?"

"I just do," he shrugged. "I will make it so."

I had to laugh. "I hope you're right."

"I usually am," he continued cockily, pulling me back to rest against his chest.

"I agree with your husband," Ares boomed from the stern of the boat. "Everything will be fine. *We* will make it so."

Charon glanced at us dismissively before shaking his head. He clearly wasn't interested or concerned with anything that we were saying. Instead, he focused on rowing the boat through the air toward a massive wall in the near distance. Above it, light glowed in the sky- a clear sign of civilization. But the wall was tall and thick and it was topped with razor sharp points.

As we drew up to it, I saw that we would have to climb over jagged rocks piled at its base to reach flat land. It certainly looked imposing. Hecate didn't hesitate.

"Come now," she urged as we climbed from the boat. "It isn't as hard as it looks."

And it wasn't. I scrambled over the sharp rocks easily enough and once I stood on land, I turned to see that everyone else was fine, as well.

Charon watched us disembark.

"I would say that I'll see you soon, but I know that I won't." He shoved away from shore and rowed in the opposite direction without looking back.

"Well, he's pleasant," Aphrodite remarked. Hecate smiled.

"He has an unpleasant job," she pointed out. "You most likely wouldn't feel very pleasant about it, either."

Aphrodite eyed the massive wall that loomed in front of us.

"As if our task is a ray of sunshine," she muttered.

"No," Hecate agreed. "It certainly is not." She squared her shoulders and glanced at me. "Ready?"

I nodded, reaching back to grasp Cadmus' hand again. He was, as always, my pillar of strength.

We marched quickly and without hesitation to the large, heavy gates. Mist rose from the ground, giving the land an ethereal glow. Wispy fingers of fog spiraled into the sky and dissipated as we pushed through them. As we drew closer to the gateway, I made out the black three-headed form of Cerberus, the guardian of the Underworld. Everyone knew... his job was to let souls in, but not to let them out. I gulped.

Hecate walked straight to him and petted the head in front of her. He lowered it so that she could access it better and she scratched him behind the ears.

"Ah, old friend," she laughed. "It is good to see you." She pulled a piece of jerky from her pocket and tossed it into the air. All three heads attempted to snap it up, ultimately causing them each to miss it.

Ortrera bent to retrieve it but when her fingers brushed it, Cerberus growled menacingly. He was the size of a large bull with three inch long razor sharp teeth. When he growled, the world listened.

My sister froze, then straightened, kicking the piece of jerky to him with her foot. He snapped it into his jaws and swallowed it without chewing. Hecate patted his stout side, seemingly unafraid.

"Cerberus, my friends and I need to enter. Will you stand aside and allow it?"

The massive beast cocked his heads and stared at her.

She nodded.

"Yes, I understand. We'll deal with Hades at that point."

Cerberus cocked his heads in the other direction and paused, apparently contemplating.

I looked at Hecate. "You can communicate with animals?"

"Only dogs," she explained. "And only because my familiar is a dog." She switched her attention back to Cerberus. "Well?"

He heaved a massive sigh and stepped to the side, his enormous jowls rippling as he breathed. His large eyes rolled over each of us, but he remained still.

Hecate motioned for us to enter, so I cautiously walked past the menacing dog and into the Underworld.

"He is concerned for us," she stated calmly, answering the unspoken question that we all had. "He knows that he is under orders to not let us leave. He doesn't want us to be trapped here."

"Us or you?" Ares asked with a small grin. "I think he wanted the rest of us for his lunch."

Hecate smiled. "He and I have known each other a long time. He is concerned for me. Since I am here with you, I cannot come and go as I normally do—at my will. The rules have changed for me."

I hadn't realized that and it brought my head up with a start.

"Well, then, I thank you for coming, Hecate. I didn't know that this was a risk for you."

She leveled an ice blue gaze at me. "It's a risk for us all, Chosen One."

A chill ran down my spine at the reminder.

"Now, then," Hecate said briskly. "You all know of the Underworld. You know the main rule. Hades protects his population fiercely. He doesn't enjoy losing numbers. We shall have to think on how we will leave. Generally, in order to leave this place, one must offer someone else in his stead. We shall have to think of a way around that, so keep that in mind as we travel. Are you ready? We will need to pass through the room of judgment first."

"The room of judgment?" I repeated in confusion. "But we aren't dead. Why must we be judged?"

She shrugged her thin shoulders.

"It is just the way it must be. No one can enter the Underworld without being judged. I have entered here thousands of times and each time, I have been judged. You will be judged in many different aspects- in relation to those who accompany you, in relation to the world in general and with regard to your own superfluous acts."

"And then what?"

She gave me a droll look. "Then you may enter."

I examined the terrain in front of us. The Underworld was actually fairly beautiful thus far. It reminded me of the Scottish Highlands. Craggy, severe hills stretched as far as I could see. Green and brown grasses waved with a crisp breeze, yellow wildflowers dotted the hillside. Muted light shone on us from an unseen source, which was strange. The Underworld was subterranean. The sun couldn't reach here, yet there was still light. I had to attribute it to magic. There was no other plausible explanation.

My mother approached me, reaching out to grasp my hand. She was calm and lovely, no evidence whatsoever that she was unnerved by our situation.

"Harmonia, there are several levels to the Underworld. Do you remember what they are?"

I wracked my brain. It was frustrating not to have full use of my memory yet. The Fates' spells were still binding and once again, I silently cursed them.

"No," I answered with slumped shoulders.

"Don't despair, sweetling," she patted my arm. "It will all come back to you after we restore Zeus. For now, let me tell you about the Underworld."

She gestured in front of us with a broad, sweeping motion.

"These are the Plains of Judgment. Nothing really resides in them. They will stretch on for miles and miles until the Lethe River. After that, we will come to the Fields of Asphodel in Erebus, which is where the neither good nor bad dwell. It is a place for the souls who did not have a spectacular life whatsoever. They did nothing of any real consequence. Hades Palace is there in that most neutral of places.

"Then, the Underworld will split into two vast directions. On one side, we will find Tartara, which is where the damned are imprisoned. On the other, we will find the Isles of the Blessed. It is a paradise, but to reach it, we would have to cross thousands of miles of oceans. And that, my dear, is your geography lesson for the day."

She grinned and I shook my head.

"Thanks."

Hecate interrupted solemnly. "There is one other main rule that you must keep in mind here- the most important. Do not eat anything in the Underworld or you will be condemned to stay. Remember Persephone."

Visions of the beautiful queen of the Underworld filled my mind for the first time in many years. I hadn't had cause to remember her until now.

The beautiful goddess was the daughter of Demeter and Zeus. Hades had cast his eye upon her long ago and desperately wanted her for his bride. He abducted her from Olympus and her mother had been so distraught that she had caused devastating droughts throughout the world. After so much mortal suffering, Zeus finally interfered and demanded that Hades return Persephone, but in the meantime, Hades had tricked her into eating Pomegranate seeds... condemning her to a life in the Underworld. Zeus once again interfered and negotiated a deal. Persephone would remain as Hades' bride, but she was free to leave for six months of the year to return to Olympus to visit her mother.

Some say that Persephone wasn't tricked at all...that she knew when she ate the seeds that she was binding herself to stay, that she did it because she had come to love the dark lord of the Underworld. No one knew for sure, but to all appearances, that did appear to be true to some extent. There were many years when Persephone did not stay in Olympus for the entire six months. She stayed for a matter of weeks before returning to her husband and his subterranean kingdom.

"So," Hecate continued, drawing my attention back to her. "Do not eat anything, no matter how hungry you become. You may drink, but no eating."

We all nodded our assent, as if we would do anything but. No one wished to be trapped here.

Ortrera examined the rolling landscape hawkishly before turning back to face the group.

"Where will we be judged? I do not see anything for miles."

"The judgment room will appear to us," Hecate said confidently. "We simply have to start walking."

"Which way?" Ares asked as he gazed across the horizon.

"It doesn't matter," Hecate answered. "Any direction will do."

So we set off. Hecate and Ares walked in the lead, followed by Cadmus, Aphrodite and me and the Amazons brought up the rear, cautiously flanking us.

"Oh, Harmonia?" Hecate called over her shoulder.

"Yes?" I answered quickly.

"There's one more thing. The magic of the gods is rendered impotent here. I thought you should know."

I shook my head wryly. "Yes, that is certainly good to know."

I took another step and almost ran smack into a brick building that was emerging abruptly from the ground. I stopped short and gaped at it with my mouth open. Cadmus grabbed my arm and pulled me backward and we stood together and watched it in amazement.

It rumbled to a stop after a few seconds and I couldn't believe my eyes. It was as though it had been there all along. The soil had settled back down around the foundation of the building as though it had never been disturbed.

The building itself was heavy and old, built from thick stone slabs and covered in green moss. It was tall, wide and formidable with a thick wooden door right in the middle. I lifted my hand and rested it on the brass door-handle.

"Should we go in?" I asked tentatively.

"Well, of course," Hecate replied. "What else would we do?"

She sidled confidently past me and opened the door, gesturing for us to enter. Ares went first, followed by the rest of the group.

"Well?" Hecate asked me with a raised eyebrow. I gulped and stepped inside, holding my husband's arm.

We were in a large darkened room with no windows. As my eyes grew accustomed to the dark, I made out several figures in the back, seated behind a table. Three people. They watched us intently as they waited for us to approach.

"Come closer," a gravelly voice instructed. "You must approach and be judged."

Cadmus wrapped his arm around my waist and whispered in my ear.

"It will be fine, my love. I promise."

A low laugh rumbled from behind the table and as we approached, I saw that it came from the man in the middle. There were three, all in long gray cloaks. The man in the middle laughed humorlessly again.

"You are fortunate," he pointed out, his gaze fastened to me. "Because you are here in a pack. Most face death alone." He stroked his long gray beard with gnarled fingers. "But you are not dead. This is most interesting. Hecate, why have you brought visitors?"

He shifted his stare to her, his eyes an icy blue, not unlike Hecate's own. She met his without flinching.

"We are in search of someone," she answered vaguely. "Several people, in fact. The Oracle of the Dead told us to begin our quest here. So, here we are. In fact, perhaps you know. Have you seen the Olympians pass through this room?"

He threw his head back and laughed again, a chilling, unnerving sound.

"If the Olympians were here, I doubt they arrived in the traditional fashion. No, we have not seen them. Until now. There are two in this room." He fixed his cold stare on my parents.

"Are you here to find your colleagues?"

Ares nodded solemnly. "Yes, we are... as well as my granddaughter. Have you seen a small girl? She has eyes the color of Harmonia's."

The man in the middle shifted his gaze back to me and locked his eyes with my own.

"Such a unique color," he observed. "But this is the first that I have seen of them."

"But the Oracle said that she was here!" I interrupted. "She must be."

"I didn't say that she wasn't," the man replied calmly. "I said that I have not seen her."

"But that's impossible," I cried. "Everyone passes through you. Everyone must be judged—"

Hecate touched cool fingers to my arm. "Harmonia," she warned. "Remain calm." She looked back to the panel of men.

"Shall we begin?"

She was brisk and businesslike. And they ignored her.

"I am Rhadamanthus," the one in the middle said coolly, then gestured to his right. "This is Minos." He gestured to his left. "And this is Aeacus. We hold your fate in our hands."

"I am not unaccustomed to having my fate rest in the hands of others," I answered.

He almost seemed to smile, but it wasn't comforting.

"Good. Then we shall begin with you. Step forward."

I moved forward, releasing my hold on Cadmus. I instantly felt alone as I stood in front of the table.

"Closer."

I took one more step.

He rose from his seat and circled the table, standing in front of me.

"May I?"

Without waiting for an answer, he lifted my hand and held it lightly within his own.

Instantly, my hand began glowing, just as if someone was holding a flashlight to my palm. Every vein in my hand was illuminated perfectly and the light quickly spread up my arm and throughout my entire body until I emitted a soft glow from head to foot.

He smiled, still holding my hand.

"You have a pure heart," he said as he closed his eyes. "There is no subterfuge or malevolence here. You are brave and true."

He reopened his eyes and dropped my hand.

"You are free to go."

"Where should I go?" I asked tremulously.

"Anywhere in the Underworld that you wish," he answered. "You have no restrictions."

He looked past me dismissively.

"Next?"

I stepped to the side as Cadmus walked forward. He was handsome as he stood quietly in front of Rhadamanthus, waiting to be judged. I realized once again that there was nothing that he wouldn't do for me. He was literally traveling to the depths of the underworld just to accompany me- to help me save our daughter. My heart overflowed with warmth, just as Rhadamanthus spoke.

"You are a worthy mate for your wife," he rasped. "Your heart is strong and brave. You do not shirk from that which you are meant to do. You may enter."

The second that he released Cadmus, my husband strode to my side.

"See?" he asked quietly. "Everything is fine. We will be on our way soon."

We watched quietly as everyone else was judged. I was not surprised at all to find that every member of my family and each Amazon warrior were judged with the same traits... brave, strong and true.

Finally, it was almost finished and only Hecate remained to be judged.

"Hecate?"

Rhadamanthus held out his hand and Hecate lightly placed hers within it, standing proudly in front of him. She had been judged by him thousands of times before so this process was routine to her.

I watched as her body lit up and every vein was exposed, the warm glow reflecting from the angles of her lovely face. Rhadamanthus grew still as he examined her and with his free hand traced a vein from her wrist to her heart.

"This is very strange, Hecate," he muttered. "Very strange. I'm sorry."

Her eyes snapped open.

"Sorry for what?" she asked curiously.

He dropped her hand quickly as if he no longer wanted to touch her and moved back behind the table, rejoining the other two.

"You have deceit and betrayal in your heart," he announced. "Your soul is not pure."

He snapped his fingers and low wails emitted from the corners of the room. Quickly, from each dark corner, shadowy figures emerged and grabbed Hecate, wrapping dark arms around her and dragging her away. A shroud of cold air fell on us all.

"This is not right!" she shrieked. "Rhadamanthus!"

He turned his head away and Hecate focused instead on me.

"Harmonia! This isn't what it seems. I need to explain..."

But they dragged her through the back wall. The second they were gone, the wailing stopped and the sudden chill lifted.

We were left staring in horror at each other.

A weight seemed to descend from my stomach into my feet. My visions had actually been true. There had actually been a traitor among us. And it had been Hecate all along.

# Chapter Four

The silence in the room was deafening. It took a minute before I felt strong enough to speak. Even still, my legs were shaking and I felt instantly numb from the magnitude of the betrayal. This couldn't be right.

"Rhadamanthus," I began hesitantly. "What did Hecate do? Who did she betray?"

He leveled his icy gaze at me and I almost didn't want to hear the answer.

"She betrayed us all. You must fix what she has done. Go quickly. You will soon reach the river Leche. You must drink from it before you continue."

"Leche?" Aphrodite piped up. "The river of forgetfulness?"

Rhadamanthus nodded. "Yes. When mortals drink from it, it erases their memories. It reacts differently in the gods. It might take some of your memories, none of them or all of them. It is dependent on you—on how strong your mind is. But regardless, you cannot continue until you have drank from it." He shrugged as he panned his gaze across each of us.

"I do hope your minds are strong," he added. "I was not forthcoming when I asked why you were here. I already knew. We've been waiting for you for a long time. Listen to me now. We generally do not offer instructions or suggestions. A person's afterlife is a private affair. However, you are not dead and this is a unique situation. You will need to attain, by any means necessary, Hades' helm of darkness. Without it, you will fail."

There was a collective gasp from my group. We were to somehow take Hades' helm of darkness from him? That was unheard of. It would be impossible.

Each of the three rulers, Poseidon, Zeus and Hades, had special tools at their disposal. Poseidon had his trident, Zeus had his lightning bolt, which he had converted into the form of a sword, and Hades had his helm of darkness.

It was a helmet enchanted with power. The holder of the helm would be granted invisibility, but more importantly, the one wearing it would be immune to the powers of the Underworld. And the Underworld was teeming with strange magic. Hades kept the helm continually by his side. There was no way that we would be able to steal it- especially without our own powers.

I shook my head slowly from side to side, so astonished that I couldn't think of what to say. My father, on the other hand, had no such trouble.

"What do you mean, we must take Hades' helm?" he thundered, the veins bulging in his forehead. "To what end? For what purpose?"

"We cannot share anymore than we already have," Rhadamanthus replied calmly. His two colleagues remained silent, their cold stares frozen on our faces. "We have already risked a great deal. Procure the helm."

With his final word, the walls around us began shaking and the panel of judges faded away. Within a few seconds, the room was gone. We were standing out in the open once again on the Plains of Judgment with the wind whipping around us. The ground beneath us was undisturbed. No one would ever know that the stone building had ever been here at all.

"I can't believe that just happened," I muttered. "Did you have any idea?" I looked to my mother. Her eyes were round as she shook her head.

"I'm still processing it myself," she admitted. "I can't believe it either. Hecate betrayed us? I can't imagine how. She annoys me at times, as you know. But I never would have thought her a traitor. I can't imagine why she would do such a thing."

"It's likely that we'll find out soon enough," Ares replied gruffly, as he reached out a meaty hand and rubbed Aphrodite's shoulder. "Don't trouble yourself with it now. One thing that I have learned in my life is that there are very few people who you can truly trust."

"Well, that's depressing," I replied grumpily, kicking at a dirt clod in front of me. In doing so, I realized that I was still barefoot. I was suddenly thankful that I had rolled up a pair of knee-high buckskin boots and tossed them into my bag. My abilities were impotent here, so I couldn't just conjure up something. I dug through my knapsack and found the soft boots, pulling them on.

Ares shrugged. "It's the truth, daughter. You will never be disappointed in someone if you don't allow it. Don't place your trust in them in the first place and they cannot let you down."

I stopped in my tracks and gazed at him, shaking my head. "I'm glad I'm not the god of war, if that is how you view the world."

He threw his head back and laughed. "As the god of war, that is how I *must* think. It must be nice to be the goddess of peace and contentment—is everything rainbows and butterflies for you?"

I rolled my eyes. "You know it is not. I have jumped in a pit of fire, lost my soul mate and family in every life for thousands of years and have recently died and come back to life. To top it all off, my daughter has been stolen from me. My life hasn't been a picnic."

He sobered. "Harmonia, we will get Raquel back. I swear it on the river Styx."

He had just uttered the most holy of oaths for an Olympian. I nodded. I knew he meant it.

"Thank you, father," I murmured, turning my attention once again to the horizon. "Where do we begin?"

"I think we should begin exactly where Rhadamanthus said," Cadmus suggested. "The river Leche."

"But where is it?" I asked. "I don't see it."The only thing in front of us was miles and miles of rolling hillside.

Ortrera stepped to my side, her long hair snapping around her shoulders in the strong wind. "Rhadamanthus said we would soon come to it," she reminded me. "I think we should just begin walking. Perhaps it will appear just as the Room of Judgment did."

"That's a good thought, daughter," Ares nodded. "Let us walk."

He strode quickly away from us down the hill without looking back. His shoulders were as broad as a doorway and he walked with purpose. My mother looked to me.

"Well, that's that, then," she smiled. "Let's go, sweetling."

The hill was steeper than it looked and it took quite a lot of work to remain balanced as we climbed down through the thick grasses. I was once again thankful for my boots. The weeds and grass were scratchy and thick. Ortrera and her warriors had boots similar to mine, so they were protected as well, but I could see red welt forming on my mother's legs. To her credit, she didn't complain.

Cadmus reached over and caught my fingers and we held hands as we picked through the bristly wildflowers. There were so many blooming that it really should smell good here, but instead, there was an underlying sulfurous smell that I couldn't quite pinpoint. I had no idea where it was coming from.

From the front, my mother and father stopped in their tracks.

"Look!" my mother exclaimed pointing. I followed her finger.

Nestled in a valley, between voluptuous green hills, a sparkling blue river gently flowed. The water was clear and clean and rushed fluidly over river rocks. At this point, we had been hiking for awhile and to be honest, I was parched. The bubble of the water was tantalizing and I found myself pulled to it as we rushed the remainder of the distance and stood at the edge.

"I'm afraid," my mother murmured as she stared into the clear depths.

"Me, too," I agreed.

My father plunged into the water without hesitation in typical Ares style. He splashed a large hand toward us, splattering us with large drops. It was frigid.

"Come on in," he cajoled. "The water's fine."

"How can you not be nervous?" Aphrodite demanded. "It could take your memories."

"It could," he acknowledged with a shrug. "But it won't."

As we all watched in trepidation, he dipped his hand in the water and drew it up to his mouth, taking a long drink. The clear liquid streamed from his chin as he drank even more. After a moment, he stopped abruptly, dropping his hand back down to his side as his gaze became glassy and vacant.

Staring at my mother intently, his whispered, "Who are you?"

She gasped. "Ares?"

"Ares?" he repeated. "Is that my name?"

My heart almost stopped beating as I stared at my mother. She returned my horrified gaze and we seemed frozen in time as we contemplated what to do.

And then my father threw his head back and started laughing.

He was kidding and I wanted to kill him.

"That is not funny!" I screeched at him as Aphrodite plunged into the river to pummel his chest with her delicate fists.

"Not funny *at all*!" Aphrodite agreed. "Are you truly unaffected?"

"Truly," he nodded. "I'm perfectly fine. Better, in fact. I feel... almost joyful."

I raised my eyebrows doubtfully. "Joyful? My father, the god of war, feels joyful?"

"Yep!" he replied, flipping onto his back and floating in the river. "Joyful. I don't know how else to describe it. I remember who I am perfectly, but I feel as though I don't have a care in the world."

"But you do," Ortrera reminded him. "We have much to care about. We don't have time to be joyful."

"You women!" he tossed over his shoulder as he swam down the stream. "Always nay-saying. You might as well try it for yourselves. You will have to anyway."

We looked at each other in hesitation. Cadmus spoke up. "I'll go first, wife."

"It doesn't really matter," I answered. "Thank you, but we're all going to have to do it. We might as well do it together."

We nervously entered the water and drew our hands to our mouths to drink.

The water was icy cold and delicious. As it trickled down my throat, I felt a strange sense of calm come over me, just as my father had mentioned. I remembered exactly who I was and who everyone else was, but I felt oddly carefree.

But even still, I remembered our mission here. I knew I had to save my daughter. Yet somehow, my sense of urgency was diminished. Even though my head knew that was not true, it was what my body felt. I would have to somehow overcome it.

"We cannot trust our own feelings now," I pointed out as I turned to Cadmus. He was already nodding. "I feel as though our purpose is no longer important, even though I know that to be untrue. Do you feel the same?"

He nodded again. "I feel incredible peace. But my memories are intact."

"Me too," Aphrodite interjected as she knelt to drink more.

I turned to ask the Amazons, but froze.

Ortrera was crouched in a combat position, her fierce face wary as she circled us. Her warriors were at attention behind her, although they looked confused by her behavior.

"Ortrera?" I asked hesitantly. I took a step toward her but she snarled so I quickly stepped back. Cadmus subtly moved to my side.

"Ortrera, do you know who I am?" I tried to keep my voice soothing and calm, but since it looked like she was about to attack me at any moment, it proved difficult. "I'm your sister. Your half-sister, actually. Do you remember?"

"Do I seem like I remember?" she snapped as she shifted her weight back and forth to each foot cautiously. "I do not remember you."

"Do you remember *you*?" I asked carefully. "Do you know who you are?"

She looked around warily and then her shoulders slumped. "No."

Her usually staid warriors suddenly looked uneasy, but they didn't falter in their defensive formation. It was admirable, really. They were prepared to defend her- to fight for her- even though she didn't remember who any of them were.

Ares had stopped swimming and was wading back toward us, a serious gleam in his dark eyes.

"Ortrera," he began. "You are my daughter. Surely you remember that."

She snorted. "Why would I remember that? I don't even remember who I am."

"You're our queen," one of her warriors said haltingly. "Do you remember *that*?"

Ortrera studied the woman who had spoken and then the rest of the strong warriors, her gaze passing over each one of them before she finally sighed.

"No," she admitted. She backed up a few steps, still on her guard. "And why should I trust any of you?"

"You shouldn't," Ares answered, his gaze glittering. "You should never truly trust anyone but yourself. That is something I've taught you since you were small. I'm the god of war. You are my daughter- a queen of the Amazon warriors and the strongest female I know. Trust your instincts. Look around you- look into our eyes. You know us."

She did as he said and examined each of us, locking eyes with every one of us in turn. But when she looked at me, her gaze remained empty and I knew she didn't know me at all. My heart sank and I moved toward her.

"Sister…"

She lunged toward me with her sword drawn. "Don't call me that!" she snapped. "I don't know you!"

I took a step back but it was useless. Ortrera was on the offensive now and kept advancing.

"I don't trust any of you!" she shouted. Cadmus moved to protect me, but I motioned him back.

"No!" I cried. "She's not herself. Do not hurt her. I have faith that she won't hurt me."

"Your faith is unfounded," she said menacingly. "There is no reason why I won't hurt you."

She swung her sword and it sliced by my ear, the blade hissing as it split the air.

I jumped back and once again motioned Cadmus and my father back.

"It will only make it worse," I said quickly.

"I don't see how this can get worse," Aphrodite replied. "Ortrera, I know you are not yourself, but if you hurt one hair on Harmonia's head, I will kill you myself. Know that."

Ortrera studied my small, slight mother and her lip curled. "Warning noted," she answered wryly.

She chose that moment to leap onto me and shoved me to the ground, the tip of her sword pressed into my chest. My heart beat against the cool blade and I tried to think- to still my racing thoughts so I could form a plan.

But nothing. I could think of nothing. So I went with instinct instead. As Ortrera shifted her weight, I used that moment to throw her off and we tumbled together, rolling over and over before I came out on top. She outweighed me, so I knew my upper-hand wouldn't last. I bend forward to try and pin her more securely and as I moved, my bloodstone fell from my shift and lay against her breast.

Her eyes instantly widened and clouded.

Her body went limp and she fell off of me to the side and rested in the grass, her chest heaving. She lay still and silent, her hands clenching and unclenching her sword. I was almost afraid to speak, but finally, I inched away just a bit and caught her eye.

"Ortrera?"

"I'm sorry," she whispered. "I know who you are. Father always loved you best."

I opened my mouth to speak, but Ares beat me to it.

"I have not," he boomed. "I love you differently, that is true. Harmonia soothes my troubled spirit, as that is her nature as the goddess of peace. You are my fierce warrior- a child after my own heart. I love each of you."

She nodded, a tear streaking out of the corner of her eye. I froze. I had never seen her cry, not in the thousands of years that we had known each other. She wiped it away impatiently.

"I'm sorry," she mumbled. "I don't know why I am emotional."

"Because we are in a difficult situation," I soothed, patting her shoulder. "It's alright. Ortrera. You weren't yourself."

She nodded as she stood. She nodded to her warriors and they once again looked comfortable as they relaxed just a little. She looked around the group.

"Now what?"

Aphrodite shrugged. "Now we are free to proceed, I think. We're none the worse for the wear even though you just tried to kill your sister."

She couldn't quite keep her grudge from her voice and I couldn't help but smile.

"Mother," I warned. "Ortrera didn't mean it. You know that."

She shrugged with her nose in the air. I shook my head, but Ortrera interrupted.

"It's alright, Harmonia. I don't blame her. But I do hope you know that I would protect you with my life."

"I know." I glanced at my mother and she looked slightly mollified. "Of course I know. You've proven yourself time and time again. And I would trust you with my life."

That seemed to make Ortrera feel better and she examined the countryside in front of us.

"I have to admit, this is not what I thought the Underworld would be like. Which way do you propose that we go?"

"That's a very good question."

As we studied the horizon, however, a cloud seemed to descend from the distance. White and jagged-edged, it seemed to drift toward us, continually changing shape as it moved.

"What's that?" Aphrodite pointed.

I squinted. "I don't know."

It got closer and as it did, we saw that it was made from butterflies…thousands of white butterflies. They fluttered in a huge circle above us before they floated down around us. They seemed to gravitate more toward Ortrera and clung to her arms and legs. She stayed frozen as she turned slightly toward me.

"What is going on?"

I shook my head slowly. "I have no idea."

I reached out a finger and a butterfly landed lightly upon it, followed by another and then another. They seemed to be everywhere- all around us.

Ortrera was almost covered with the insects. They were pretty little things, but they were tangled in her hair, clinging to her arms and fluttering around her legs. And then suddenly, they weren't. They formed a cloud once again and hovered directly in front of us.

"It's almost like they want us to follow them," Aphrodite pondered. At her words, they moved forward a bit.

"I think you're right," Cadmus agreed, taking my hand and swinging my knapsack onto his shoulder. "I think that's exactly what they want."

"So we should just follow a big swarm of bugs?" Ortrera asked incredulously.

Ares rolled his eyes. "Daughter, you should know by now, nothing is what it seems in the Underworld. Or anywhere else, for that matter."

He looked down at Aphrodite's scratched up legs. She had thin streaks of blood from a few of the deeper scratches running down her slender calves.

"Do those hurt?" he demanded.

But before she could even answer, he had snatched her up and slung her onto his back, as easily as Cadmus had swung my knapsack. She rested her face against his stout back, clearly exhausted. I felt sorry for her. This was not something that my mother was accustomed to. But then again, neither were the rest of us.

"Let's go!" he called over his shoulder as he began marching up the next hill with Aphrodite on his back and the butterflies leading the way.

Cadmus looked to me. "Would you like for me to carry you?"

I laughed wearily. "I wish. But no. You need your strength, too."

He looked at me in mock outrage. "You think I'm so weak that I can't carry you?"

"Of course not. I know you can. But we don't know what is coming and I want you at your best when we face it. Raquel needs you."

That thought sobered him up immediately and he nodded. "Raquel needs us both. And we'll be there. I promise you that, my love."

I leaned up and pressed my lips to his, savoring the warm, familiar kiss. The unknown was scary, but facing it with Cadmus made it more palatable.

"Ready?" He raised a dark eyebrow.

"As I'll ever be."

He wrapped his arm around my waist and we followed the others into the fields of the Underworld.

# Chapter Five

Erebus was such a neutral place that it was easy to forget where we were as we traveled. This part of the Underworld wasn't foreboding in the slightest. It was breezy, earthy and seemingly normal.

It was also very large. The flower dotted fields were so vast that we seemed to walk forever. One strange thing about the Underworld was that there was no sun to gauge the passage of time. The strange muted light that surrounded us stayed the same. It didn't fade or brighten, so time seemed to run together.

Finally, after walking the steep hills for hours, I couldn't take it anymore- at least not today. My calves were literally trembling from exhaustion and I stopped in my tracks.

"We've got to stop," I called to Ares who was still briskly leading the pack with my mother on his back. Aphrodite had actually fallen asleep against his shoulder blades, her arms dangling loosely around his neck. I envied her. I was dead on my feet.

"Why?" he asked in surprise, turning.

"Because I'm going to fall down any minute," I snapped. "Not all of us are machines like you."

He raised a dark eyebrow. "I'm not a machine. Sue me for being fit."

I rolled my eyes. I knew that I was being cranky, but I just couldn't help it. I had never been so tired in my life. Cadmus wrapped me in his arms and I buried my face against his chest, inhaling his delicious scent. He always smelled like the outdoors-clean and musky. I was so weary and so comfortable in this spot, that I knew I would fall asleep right here if I didn't move.

I pulled away reluctantly.

"We've got to find somewhere to sleep."

"Where do you suggest?" Ortrera asked as she looked over the countryside. "There's nothing but empty fields for miles and miles."

"Well, that could be a problem," I acknowledged.

"But not an insurmountable one," my father added. "Look."

In the near distance to our right, there was a cluster of large boulders in the juncture of two hills. It would provide some semblance of protection from the rolling fields. I didn't hesitate. I simply started walking toward it. The butterflies fluttered in a billowing cloud above us and they followed us overhead as we moved.

The open space was misleading. Even though it looked fairly close, it still took us an hour or so to reach the boulders. But once we did, we were pleasantly surprised. It was a cave.

Out here in the middle of nowhere, a cave stood alone. Ares slid Aphrodite gently to the ground and then pushed ahead, joined by Cadmus and Ortrera as they plunged inside the dark depths of the doorway. My mother and I stood quietly with the Amazons as we waited for the verdict.

It came quickly.

Ares poked his head out of the doorway. "It's safe. Come on in."

My mother and I glanced at each other warily, but we didn't hesitate as we followed them in. We were simply too tired to care. And as we entered the small cave, it was immediately evident that there wasn't anything to worry about, anyway.

It was one room and barren. There was nothing in it at all but a few scattered pebbles and a tiny clear pool of water. It wasn't fed by a spring, so I decided that it must bubble up directly from the ground. As we stepped in, the temperature immediately dropped a few degrees as we were surrounded by the cool stone.

I took a deep breath as I looked around. There was evidence of an old campfire in the center because the ground was blackened and there was a pile of partially burned logs. So, clearly this was a cave that was used by others at times. We'd have to hope that they didn't choose to return tonight- because I was just too tired to defend it against intruders.

Ares rubbed Aphrodite's arms gently as he gazed into her eyes.

"Are you alright?" He studied her face as he waited for an answer. She was unusually pale so it was obvious that she was exhausted. She was also unusually quiet, which was even more of a red-flag. Silence was something that simply wasn't in her molecular make-up.

She nodded. "I don't know why I feel so tired. I'm just... wiped out."

He examined her carefully, running his hands over her arms and brushing her honey-colored hair back from her face. "You seem to be fine," he replied cautiously.

She nodded. "I know. There shouldn't be anything wrong with me. I haven't been injured. I'm just so tired."

I watched her in concern. "Mother, you should lie down. You look like you are ready to fall down." She nodded in agreement, weariness etched on her exquisite face. She had never seemed as delicate as she did right now.

I grabbed her knapsack and rummaged through it, finding a soft wrap. I wound it around her shoulders and helped her settle onto the hard ground as comfortably as I could make it. I sat beside her quietly with her head in my lap, stroking her arm as I watched Ares and Cadmus talk quietly by the cave entrance. Aphrodite was asleep within a minute.

I glanced in alarm at my father.

"Ares!"

He turned to me questioningly, but when he saw Aphrodite asleep already, he rushed to my side and scooped her into his arms. He settled with his back against the stone wall as he cradled her to his chest, allowing her to sleep in comfort.

"Is she alright?" I asked quietly.

He nodded, although his face wasn't as confident.

"She's just tired, daughter. She's not accustomed to extended hikes in the Underworld."

"Okay," I answered quietly. I prayed that he was right. My mother's face was slack and innocent in her sleep and it was hard to imagine that anything could be wrong with her. So, I put it out of my mind.

Moving to Cadmus' side, I snuggled against him. "We should sleep, husband."

He looked at me affectionately. "You go first, my love. Someone needs to keep watch."

Ortrera piped up.

"Cadmus, my warriors and I will take turns. You should attend to Harmonia. She looks as exhausted as Aphrodite."

"Are you certain?" he raised a dark eyebrow.

"Of course," she nodded. "I'm not even tired."

The lines of exhaustion on her face belied her words, but it would be useless to argue. The Amazons took pride in their fierce fortitude.

"Very well," he patted her toned shoulder. "But should you need me, let me know."

She nodded silently, taking her place at the door. She never asked her warriors to do anything that she herself wouldn't do. So it was just like her to take the first watch.

I retreated to a back corner and tried to make a comfortable sleeping area out of the contents of my knapsack. The end result was no feather mattress, but it would do. Cadmus plunked down on it first, stretching his long legs out and opening his arms.

"I've been waiting all day for this," he grinned, his teeth brilliantly white. "Come here."

I gladly sank to the floor and folded into his embrace. He clutched me to his chest and I reveled in his strength. I had never felt safer anywhere than I did in his arms. It was like home to me.

"I love you more than life, Harmonia," he murmured against the top of my head. "I would move the heavens and the earth for you. I hope you know that."

I nodded. Of course I knew it. He had killed dragons for me.

"Cadmus, if it wasn't for you, I don't know how I would have made it through everything that I have. You've kept me strong and have given me a reason to keep trying. You are my strength. I thank you for that."

"Oh, my sweet," he brushed his lips against the side of my neck before pulling me even closer. "You are stronger than all of us. You just don't realize it. Sleep now, though. You need the rest. Do not worry. I'll protect you with my life."

I nodded as my eyes fluttered closed with a will of their own. I would have liked to stay awake just a little longer, to enjoy being close to my husband. We had not been able to enjoy intimacy of this sort lately- everything had been so chaotic. But my body wouldn't hear of it. I was too tired to stay awake.

Before I knew it, I was standing with Ahmose. His black robes billowed around him and he was staring at me intently. I looked around in confusion before realization set in and I groaned. I was dream-walking. My least favorite thing to do.

I sighed and turned to him. "Why are you here, Ahmose? I should be sleeping soundly. I'm more exhausted than I have ever been."

"Of course you are," he agreed, gazing at me sympathetically. "More than you even know."

"What do you mean by that?"I narrowed my eyes suspiciously. His own were glinting with hidden knowledge. I had seen that look from him a million times. "What is it?"

"Ah, Harmonia. You know that nothing can ever be easy for you."

"And nothing ever is," I scowled. "But what are you speaking of right now?"

I was impatient and I instantly regretting snapping at him. He had died for me before after all. "I'm sorry. What are you talking about?"

"I'm concerned for you, Harmonia, but I'm even more worried for your mother. You both are going to have to take great care. You're in danger there."

I rolled my eyes. "We're in the Underworld. We're all in danger."

"It's more than that," he continued patiently. "You and your mother are goddesses who live on positive energy. You require peacefulness to feed your spirit and your mother requires the energy of love. You're currently in a place where that kind of energy simply doesn't exist. Erebus is neutral. The only emotional energy you will receive there will be from the few people surrounding you. It's not enough. Particularly for your mother- Love is a stronger energy and without it…well, your mother is in danger."

Shock hit me like a wave. Of course- it made perfect sense. No wonder my mother and I could hardly stay awake. Our energy was being drained from us.

"You're right," I whispered. "She was very weak tonight. She could barely stay awake and frankly, neither could I. What can we do?"

He stared at me, his black eyes glinting. "You can leave. It's the only thing that will ultimately help you. In the meantime, I sent you butterflies. Did you receive them? They bring with them energy from the mortal world. It's not enough to make you feel normal, but it is enough to keep you alive. Your energy will be recharged in Hades' palace but once you leave there, you will be in peril once again. You must hurry and return to the Spiritlands or there will be dire consequences."

"Why didn't someone tell us this before?" I demanded. "This would have been good to know."

"Would it have stopped you from going?" he answered calmly and I swallowed. Of course it would not have and he knew it.

"See?" he answered. "It wouldn't have mattered. But I am telling you now."

"So, you're telling me that bugs will keep us alive?"

He stared at me. "They are ethereal creatures, Harmonia. They will keep you alive. And when you drain their energy, I will send you more."

"Why are things surrounding me always so strange?" I demanded. "I feel like I'm Alice in Wonderland half of the time."

"It is what it is," he shrugged. He was in his original form right now, ancient and stooped. His head was shaved bald and his hands were gnarled and old, his fingernails so long that they curled into his palm. I had always wondered why he chose this form- when he could appear as anything or anyone that he wished. But that was neither here nor there right now.

"How are things there?" I asked, changing the subject. "They have told us here that Hecate betrayed us and they dragged her away. Do you know anything about that?"

He looked away. "Not enough to be of help, but I'll continue to hunt. Eris and I have found nothing of use for you," he admitted. "We have searched through the old writings with Medea and Circes and there is simply nothing of consequence."

"Why is Eris trying to be helpful?" I was instantly suspicious of my old nemesis. She and I were polarized goddesses. She was the goddess of strife and discord and I was the goddess of peace. We weren't meant to get along, yet in Camelot she had uncharacteristically assisted us. I had not yet had a chance to try to figure that out.

"Eris has her own motives," Ahmose admitted. "And they might actually be of assistance."

"Her motives?" I raised an eyebrow.

He nodded. "She has not miraculously turned good, of course. She has long been in love with Alexi. She wants to find a way to save his soul."

"Alexi?" I gasped. He had been the lapdog of the Fates for as long as I could remember. He had done their bidding for them and was currently confined in the dungeons of Zeus' palace. No one had known what to do with him, so they were holding him for Zeus to deal with. It seemed like the fair thing to do.

Ahmose nodded. "And do you remember who Alexi actually is?"

I wracked my brain, but came up empty. All I could remember was how he was now- dispassionate and cold- because the Fates' had taken his soul. They had sent him to deal with me after they had disposed of Ahmose.

"He's the son of Alecto." Ahmose waited for that to click with me, which it quickly did.

Alecto was one of the Erinyes…otherwise known as the Furies or the Avengers. They acted in much the same way as the Keres, but they did it in the Underworld. They tortured prisoners in the Dungeon of the Damned in Tartara. They worked for Hades.

I sucked in a breath and Ahmose nodded. "Do you see where I am going with this?"

"I think so," I replied quietly. "Alecto will not enjoy hearing that her son's soul has been taken."

"I'm sure she already knows," Ahmose answered. "But her hands are tied because she cannot leave the Underworld. But you are there now. You can talk with her about this…perhaps bargain with her, if you must. It is an angle that might be at your disposal."

I nodded. "I'll keep that in mind."

"But right now," he continued. "You must get to Hades palace as soon as possible. Your mother's strength will not hold for much longer."

"Yes," I agreed. "I know that you are right."

"Then go," he instructed, pointing with a long, twisted finger.

And I was awake. My eyes opened to find the cave exactly like it had been when I went to sleep, except that another Amazon had taken Ortrera's place as guard. The white butterflies were plastered against the walls of the cave, their delicate wings moving slightly as they waited.

"Do you feel better?" Cadmus asked quietly.

I was still lying on his chest and it didn't look like he had slept much. He was still beautiful, of course, but his face was weary. His chocolate eyes didn't shine as much as they normally did. I reached up to brush my fingers against his strong jaw line, where his rough stubble snagged at my fingers. We were all a little worse for the wear.

"I'm fine for now," I answered. "But Ahmose came to me while I slept and I learned a couple of interesting things."

"Like what?" Ares asked from across the room. Sound carried easily in this cavern. I sat up so that I was facing everyone.

"My mother and I will continue to be drained of energy," I announced. "Because we thrive on positive energy and there is none of that here. Aphrodite will be more strongly affected than me, because love is a stronger emotion than peace. But both of us will be affected until we leave. Ahmose sent the butterflies from the mortal world- they'll bring us energy, but they'll simply keep us alive. They aren't able to do much more than that. Ahmose says that we can recharge at Hades Palace."

Ares was already moving, lying Aphrodite on the ground as he stood.

"Well, let's move then."

"There's more." I leveled my gaze at him. Ares stilled and listened as I explained about Alexi. He stared thoughtfully at me when I finished.

"That makes perfect sense," he admitted. "I don't know why we didn't figure it out before. I've seen the way she lingers around him whenever she can. We'll keep that in our back pocket for later use."

I crossed the cave to kneel next to my mother. I shook her arm gently, but she didn't stir. Her face was still deathly pale and she didn't respond to my attempts to wake her.

"This is bad, Ares!" I cried as I desperately tried to rouse her. He bent and scooped Aphrodite up once again.

"It will be fine!" he decreed as he strode towards the hills. "But as I said, we need to move."

He didn't dally. By the time I had packed up our things as quickly as I could and exited the little cave, Ares was a small dot in the distance, surrounded by the billowing white cloud of butterflies. Ortrera looked at me ruefully.

"He's your father."

I shook my head. "Oh, he's mine when he's difficult?"

She grinned. "I'm glad you agree."

We laughed and started out across the field in pursuit. But I had only taken a few steps before I felt exhaustion set in myself and I couldn't help but worry. How would I find Raquel if simply being here might kill me?

I had no sooner had the thought before Cadmus swept me into his arms.

"You've got to conserve your strength," he instructed. I didn't argue. I rested my head against him as he carried us with strong steps across the Asphodel Fields of Erebus.

# Chapter Six

We knew when we were close. As if we had crossed an invisible boundary, the ethereal white butterflies fell dead from the sky.

Thousands of them rained down on us and fluttered lifelessly to the ground.

I met Ortrera's eyes.

"This doesn't bode well," I muttered.

"Chin up, sister," she answered as she examined the broad horizon. "We don't know what it means."

"Oh, I think we do," Ares said. He was not even out of breath even though he had carried my mother for miles. "It means that Hades is near."

"He has something against butterflies?" I asked.

"He has something against anything beautiful, if he is not able to own it. He sucks the beauty right out of it."

I gulped as I glanced at the insects. And Ares was right. As we crested the hill that we were climbing, Hades' palace loomed in front of us. The butterflies had led us straight to it.

It was enormous. And it wasn't exactly what you would expect the god of the Underworld to live in. It was actually quite beautiful and only slightly on the gothic side. It had spires and columns and thousands of windows. There was no fire or brimstone in sight.

But there was an army.

In perfectly formed rows, thousands of haggard soldiers lined up in front of the palace. They filled acres and acres. They were an impressive sight, especially considering that they seemed to be undead.

Their skin was gray, their cheeks hollow. Their eyes were cold and flat. They stood at attention, completely still with their eyes fixed straight ahead. A drastic chill emanated from them and I shivered as we grew closer.

We moved cautiously through them and they didn't budge an inch or even break rank to look at us. They allowed us to enter the perimeter and approach the palace.

"What does this mean?" I whispered to Cadmus.

"It means that we're expected," he answered calmly.

The god of the Underworld was waiting for us? It wasn't exactly a comforting thought. I focused on staying calm as we approached and when we reached the massive gates, Cadmus stood me on my feet and I took his arm. Keeping one hand on his palpable strength was truly comforting. I hoped it would leak into me by osmosis.

"We're here to see Hades," Ares demanded of the guard.

The undead guard didn't meet my father's eyes, he simply nodded once curtly and the gates opened. We were definitely expected.

Ares led the way across the drawbridge-like entry and into the palace.

The entry way opened up into a cavernous foyer made from glistening onyx, polished to a high shine. The second we entered, I began to feel better, as though my strength was being returned to me. I quickly looked to my mother. She was coming around also, opening her eyes and lifting her head from my father's chest. I breathed a sigh of relief.

This room was empty of any furniture but for a large wall of clocks to my right. There were hundreds of them, showing the times of everywhere from Sidney to Juneau. I was staring quizzically at them when a low voice came from the shadows.

"Why do I care, right? Time does not exist here."

I whipped my head around to find a tall, slender man emerging from the darkness. It had to be Hades. I knew from simply looking at him that it could be no one else.

He had shoulder length dark hair, black eyes and golden skin. And he wasn't what I expected. He was… handsome and young. He had the physical appearance of someone in their thirties. He wore black leather pants and an unbuttoned white flowing shirt. A dark cloak was casually thrown over his shoulders but it didn't conceal anything. His stomach was flat and sculpted.

From all appearances, Hades could have been a rock star. There was a brooding air of something romantically dark surrounding him. It immediately stood all of my nerve-endings at attention in an almost pleasing way. Something about him screamed dangerous, but deep inside, I liked it. And that put me instantly on guard.

He circled around to stand in front of us, but his gaze was fixed on me. The fact that I was the Chosen One had never been so glaringly obvious. I felt like the prey of a lion as he quietly examined me and I subconsciously hid my birthmark with my other hand.

"Harmonia," he smiled. And he had a beautiful smile.

He reached out and picked up my hand, drawing it to his lips. The imprint from the touch of his lips lingered, almost buzzing with electricity even as he released my hand and I dropped it back to my side.

"It is a pleasure to finally meet you," he said as his dark eyes flitted over my body. I had the conflicting urges to both cover up and to step closer to him. What the hell was wrong with me? It was as though he literally exuded magnetism. I now understood how men felt around Aphrodite. It was an almost uncontrollable urge.

I glanced at my husband to find his jaw clenched. He could sense it, too, the effect Hades was having on me. I reached over and grasped his hand. Hades glanced down, but didn't acknowledge that he'd seen my gesture.

"I'm Hades," he offered casually with another smile…as though he hadn't just announced that he was the King of the Underworld. I wouldn't know how to begin to classify his demeanor. He was confident, yet not brash. In fact, he was almost understated. He was quiet-mannered, yet he possessed a definite air of danger. I knew without question that whatever else he was, he was a threat to me on many, many levels.

And he knew it.

His eyes assessed mine, almost as though he was reaching into my soul to examine it as well. He moved to circle me, standing behind me as he leaned in to murmur into my ear.

"You're a light, little Harmonia," he breathed. "A pure and innocent light. We've needed someone like you for a long while."

"Don't get used to it," Cadmus snapped, pulling me closer to him. "We won't be staying."

Hades looked to him without concern. "Will you not? There are not many ways for you to leave," he remarked, before he looked to my mother.

"Aphrodite, I do hope you are feeling better?"

My father had put her down and she was standing at his side, grasping his elbow. She did look immensely better. Color had returned to her cheeks and her eyes were once again spitting fire. She tilted up her nose.

"I'm well, thank you," she sniffed. I hid my smile. She was indeed better. Her spunk had returned and it was obvious that she was not happy with this entire state of affairs.

Hades looked mildly amused at her behavior. He nodded with a small smile and spread his hands wide at his sides.

"Come," he gestured toward the hall. "I have prepared a feast for you. You must join us. Persephone is waiting…and she is not what would call patient."

He turned and led the way, walking fluidly into the hall. He almost seemed to glide.

"As if we would eat," Ares muttered as they followed. I could hear Hades chuckle, but he said nothing in reply.

Cadmus leaned toward me, brushing his lips across my cheek bone. "Everything will be fine, Harmonia." He was intent and he believed it. I so hoped he was right.

"I know," I answered.

We continued down a long marble hallway. On either side, framed artwork hung on the pristine walls. Priceless, original pieces. I recognized Picasso, Rembrandt, Van Gogh, Degas, Matisse. As Hades turned to wait for us, he followed my gaze.

"I do love the art of the mortals," he said. "It's as though their fleeting lives allow them to truly capture beauty."

"Well, your paintings are certainly beautiful," I agreed.

He dipped his head slightly in acceptance of my compliment. "Yet their beauty is far outshined by your own."

His demeanor was fascinating and I found myself sucked in by it. He was genteel and sophisticated, sexy and dark. I had to continually remind myself who I was dealing with and I gave him a wide berth as I passed by him. He fell into step behind us and his presence was enormous. I felt him one step behind me even without looking.

The hall led us to a beautiful dining room filled with sparkling chandeliers, gleaming silver elaborate draperies and flickering candles. A long table was filled with elegant displays of food and sparkling pitchers of wine. At the far end of the table, Persephone waited, watching us as we entered.

She was beautiful. Not as beautiful as my mother, but then no one was. One of Aphrodite's gifts was in being the epitome of beauty to every eye that beheld her. She was each person's personal vision of perfection. There was no competing with that.

But Persephone gave her a run for her money.

She was curvy and her breasts spilled over the top of her perfectly fitted purple satin gown. Chunky necklaces and bracelets of amethyst adorned her neck and wrists, which made her dark blue eyes appear purple. Her russet colored hair was piled on top of her head with tendrils escaping to curl around her face. She was lovely and young, although the wisdom in her eyes betrayed her age. She also had a sharpness about her. It was evident that she had seen many things throughout her life here in the Underworld.

She stood as we entered and Hades crossed the room to her side, kissing her briefly on the cheek. There was appreciation in his eyes when he appraised her appearance. It was a well-known fact that he was in love with his wife.

"My wife, Persephone," he introduced. "Persephone, we are honored to host Harmonia, Cadmus, Ares, Aphrodite, Ortrera and her fierce Amazon warriors. I wonder what we did to receive such an honor?"

He turned his gaze back to us in question.

"Well?" he asked smoothly. "Why have we been blessed with your presence?"

He was perfectly calm as he slid Persephone's chair in for her and then turned to us, waiting for an answer.

Aphrodite gave him one.

"You know why we're here!" she spit in agitation. "We're here because somewhere in this godforsaken place, you have Harmonia's daughter. And perhaps you have the other Olympians, as well! Where have you put them?"

Hades chuckled darkly as he walked toward us.

"And why would you assume that?"

As he drew nearer, I saw the danger glittering in the depths of his dark eyes and it made me want to retreat. I innately knew that I had never been in the presence of someone as dangerous as Hades. He reminded me of a coiled up cobra, deadly and poised to strike.

"The Oracle of the Dead told us to come here," I answered quietly, calming standing my ground even though I wanted to flee. He was dangerous on many levels. "She said that we would find all that we seek in the Underworld. But you know that, don't you? You've been expecting us. Everyone here is expecting us."

"Perhaps," he conceded, examining me. "Am I correct in assuming that none of you will be eating from this delicious feast?"

I nodded curtly. "You are correct."

He smiled again, a breath-taking smile. His teeth were brilliantly white in contrast with his dark hair and golden skin. I once again had to suppress my surprise. He was a beautiful man and I hadn't been expecting that.

"Then perhaps I could have a word with you, alone?" He glanced at the rest of the group. "I'm sure Aphrodite should rest. And Persephone, perhaps you could keep the rest of our visitors entertained?"

"Of course, my love," she nodded. "I would be happy to."

She rose from her seat without eating and swayed toward me. But she didn't even look at me. Instead, she fixed her gaze on Cadmus and took his arm.

"We have many lovely things in our home. I so rarely get a chance to show them off. Please, come with me."

Cadmus looked to me, his forehead wrinkled in concern. Here in the Underworld, I wasn't able to read his mind but I already knew what he was thinking. He didn't want to leave me alone with Hades. And to be honest, I didn't want him to. My heart was racing already. But I didn't have a choice. Hades might know something about Raquel. In fact, I was fairly certain that he did. And I knew that he wouldn't share anything if we didn't play by his rules.

So, I sighed and nodded. "It's fine. I'll be fine."

Cadmus stared into my eyes. "Are you certain?"

"Of course," I answered with as much bravado as I could muster. "Hades just wants to talk to me. It's alright."

Persephone laughed, her voice tinkling like expensive crystal bells. "What harm could come from a conversation?"she laughed. "Truly. She will be fine." She looped her other arm through Aphrodite's.

"We have so much to catch up on," Persephone murmured to my mother. "Please, tell me everything."

She led them away and out the door. Cadmus glanced worriedly over his shoulder as they left and I smiled at him in reassurance. It was an assurance that I didn't feel, but hopefully he didn't know that. The Amazons trailed behind them and as the last one turned the corner, Hades turned to me.

"I've known for a long time that this day would come," he confided in me, his voice like velvet. I honestly could listen to his voice forever. It was like creamy caramel drizzling over my entire body. It was that smooth. I shook my head. Why was I dwelling on that? What was wrong with me?

"You have?" I studied his handsome face. He didn't seem worried or concerned. Like everyone else, he was simply expectant. "And now that it is here?"

"Now that it is here, I find that I do not know what to say."

He laughed softly as he picked up my hand and turned it over to trace my birthmark with his fingers. His touch was electrifying and I wondered if it was that way for everyone or if he and I just had a strange connection. I tried to calm my breathing.

He bent his dark head to examine my mark more closely.

"This looks painful," he said as he traced the blackened outline of the Phoenix. "Why did they do this to you?"

His eyes held sympathy and it appeared to be genuine. Every trace of danger that had been there only a few minutes ago was gone and now, he somehow seemed kind. But I knew better than to trust it. I pulled my hand away.

"I do not know," I admitted. "But it doesn't hurt any longer."

He shook his head. "It is a pity that they marred even a fraction of your perfection."

"I am not perfect."

"That is debatable," he replied softly and I couldn't help but watch his perfectly formed lips as he spoke. What had he done to me? Why did I feel such a pull toward him? I had never experienced anything like it. Even with… Cadmus. My soul mate. I cleared my throat.

"Can you help me find my daughter?"

He studied me for a moment, cocking his head just a little, causing his dark hair to tumble into his eye. He tossed it out of the way.

"Perhaps," he answered. "But what would do for me in return?"

Panic took off in my chest like a flock of startled birds. There wasn't anything I wouldn't do for Raquel. But here in the Underworld with Hades, I felt as though my very soul was on the line. And I knew that more than likely, that was exactly the case.

"What do you mean?" I whispered, taking a step back.

He circled around me, putting both hands on my shoulders and leaning in to speak softly into my ear. His breath was warm on my cheek.

"I think you know what I mean," he answered. "I want you to stay here… with me. Is that too high a price for your daughter?"

His voice was almost intoxicating, as if it was caressing my face as he spoke. I almost leaned into it before I realized what I was doing. I blinked hard and yanked away.

"What are you doing to me?" I demanded. "Stay there. Don't come any closer." He laughed, but remained motionless as I requested.

"We have a connection. Don't you see?"He watched me from a distance as I backed slowly away.

"We don't have a connection, Hades. You just want what you cannot have. I think you must get bored down here and this is how you bring excitement into your life."

Before I could say another word, he blurred into motion and was at my side in an instant. I had forgotten… I might not have goddess abilities here, but he certainly retained his. I cringed away as he pulled me to him, sliding his hands against my back.

"You think that was excitement?" he asked innocently. "I think not."

He pressed his lean form against me, running his hands along my sides, trailing his fingers upward along the sides of my breasts. My nerve endings were on fire. I inhaled sharply and looked away.

"Now we're getting somewhere," he continued softly, pushing the hair away from my neck. "I can see your pulse beat here," he said as he lightly caressed my neck. "You seem afraid."

"I'm not afraid," I answered. "But I am married and I am not enjoying this. You need to stop."

"There's something you should know about me," he said as he looked into my eyes. "I am the King of the Underworld. And one of my gifts is knowing when someone is lying. You are lying. You are enjoying this right now. Perhaps it is deep down in the murky part of your soul where you hide bad things away, but nevertheless… you are enjoying this."

And by the gods, he was right. Everywhere he had touched me was tingling with pleasure and it turned my stomach. But it didn't mean that it wasn't true.

Even still, I knew it wasn't my fault. Hades had done something... enchanted me somehow. Perhaps this strange magnetism was one of his gifts, just like Aphrodite. I was in love with my husband with every cell in my body. Somehow, some way, Hades had turned my body into a traitor. I wrenched away from him, shaking as I stood several feet away.

"Please," I pleaded. "Please. Do you know where Raquel is?"

He nodded seriously.

"Yes."

My heart rate picked up and I stepped toward him once again.

"Where?" I heard the desperation in my voice myself, but it didn't matter. He already knew that I was desperate to find her. I couldn't hide that.

"You know the price," he said simply.

I closed my eyes and sagged against the wall dejectedly. How was I ever going to save her? Would I really have to sacrifice my soul to do it?

"Harmonia, come with me," Hades murmured from two inches away. I opened my eyes hesitantly. He had silently moved to my side and reached to take my elbow. "There is something that might help you decide."

"There is no decision," I snapped. "I am not staying with you. You have a wife. You love her dearly. Why would you want me anyway?"

He looked at me in surprise. "Of course I love Persephone. What does that have to do with anything?"

I stared back in exasperation. "It has everything to do with it! You have a wife, I have a husband. *I am not staying here with you.*"

He threw his head back and laughed.

"Ah, Harmonia. I should have expected nothing less from you and it is so delightful and refreshing." He sobered as he studied me once more and I felt as though he was looking into my soul.

"But I will have you."

He began strolling, lightly grasping my elbow. "Come. I must show you something."

I was nervous, but I didn't have a choice. Although his touch on my arm was light, it had bound me to him with invisible steel. I found my feet moving along with his, even though I wasn't propelling them myself. Strange.

We crossed through the lavish banquet hall and out onto a manicured terrace. Exotic flowers grew around the stone tiles of the courtyard and I inhaled them. The heady scent was delicious, like nothing I had ever smelled before…like a combination of peaches, roses, honeysuckle and jasmine. It was heavy and lingered on my tongue.

In the center of the courtyard was a bubbling fountain. I could tell that it was very old. Three large layered bowls were balanced on a stone pedestal with water pouring from the top down. Hades led me to it.

"This is the Fountain of Truth," he explained. "Drink from it and it will reveal parcels of truth to you, things that have happened or things that will be. There is nothing else like it in all the world."

"Can it help me find Raquel?" I turned my eyes to him. He shrugged.

"I do not know what it will reveal to you. Would you like to find out?"

I looked at it again. It seemed innocuous enough. It was only water. Right? What harm could it do? I nodded.

"Alright."

He picked up a nearby bronze cup and dipped it in the bottom bowl of the fountain. He handed it to me, stepping back to allow me to drink. I sniffed at it. It had no smell. It appeared to truly be water.

I took a tentative sip. Then another. Nothing happened.

And then my eyes clouded over and the present ceased to exist. I was staring through murky fog at what seemed to be the past. Zeus and Cadmus walked the cobblestone streets of Olympus, speaking in earnest.

"You must," Zeus implored my husband. He was frightening with his insistence, his silver eyes drilling a hole in Cadmus. Zeus clearly wanted something very badly from him. "It is the only way to protect her."

The hair on the back of my neck stood up. *Me?*

Cadmus stared absently at the horizon of the bustling city. "I do not think I can. It is not right."

"Not right?" Zeus boomed and everyone on the streets around him drew to a stop, staring in apprehension. He immediately calmed and dropped his voice again.

"Why do you think we are in this position? Because of the treachery and deceit of the Fates. They think to overthrow me. I have heard of their plans.

"In readiness for it, I must put safeguards into place to protect us all, although I know you are only concerned for your wife. So know this, this is the only way to protect her. Otherwise, they will eventually hunt her down and eliminate her, because they know that she will stand in their way."

Zeus' face was thunderous even though his voice was now calm.

"I knew this long ago. Why do you think that I allowed Hephaestus to use my own blood when he created the necklace for Harmonia? Because my blood will be the key to save us and Harmonia must be the one to hold it.

"You must become mortal, along with Harmonia. It is the best way to hide you. You will be reborn, life after life, until the time comes that they manage to trick me. At that time, you will return and right it. As the goddess of peace, Harmonia is the Chosen One. She will bring peace to Olympus. But the only way to ensure that is to hide her from the Fates."

I froze, sucking in a ragged breath. Surely not. Surely not. *Surely NOT.* Cadmus couldn't have known all along. He couldn't have been part of the decision that imprisoned me in mortal form for thousands of years. Please god. Please, please god. No.

Cadmus stared at Zeus seriously, clearly weighing the situation carefully.

"If I agree, what will happen?"

The corner of Zeus' mouth twitched, but he did not smile. "If you agree, then I will allow you to accompany her, to be with her in every lifetime. If you do not, I'll send her alone."

Cadmus nodded seriously. "Very well, then. I don't see that I really have a choice."

"You're correct. You do not."

"How will we know when it is time to return and fight? We'll be in mortal form. We'll have no abilities to use."

Zeus pondered that for a scant moment. "I will send my two advisors, Ahmose and Annen, to keep track of you in each life. They will guide you and let you know when it is time. I'll assign Annen to you and Ahmose to Harmonia."

It felt like my heart froze in my chest. Zeus had sent Annen and Ahmose. Zeus himself, not the Fates. Everything that I thought I knew was raveling apart.

Cadmus nodded in agreement.

"Fine," he replied curtly. "I'll go along with this. But we cannot tell her. It will break her heart."

The world seemed to stop and whirl together at the same time. The colors of the garden around me bled into one another and I put out a hand to steady myself. Hades' took my hand.

"He betrayed you," he whispered. "He lied to you."

No matter how much I wished it wasn't true, it was. The idea that they purposely cast me into mortal form for so long was bad enough… but to lie to me about it? That was heinous.

And it had been Cadmus' idea.

# Chapter Seven

Confusion, combined with anger, clouded my mind with dark shades of red.

"I don't understand," I murmured. "I'm confused. Zeus cast me into mortal form? And then what happened?"

Hades watched me calmly, his handsome face sympathetic.

"Well, obviously, the Fates found you."

"Yes. And?"

"They turned the plan around. The plan had apparently been to keep you safe and hidden in the mortal world until the Fates had executed their plan to take over Olympus. Once that happened, Annen and Ahmose were supposed to bring you back to Olympus where you could fight for everything that was right and good… and all that." He shrugged dismissively. "But you know what they say about the best laid plans."

"What happened?" I demanded. "How did it go wrong?"

"Me," he replied simply and without remorse.

"You?" My voice was small.

"Yes, me. The Fates' plan was not going to work. I stepped in and offered my assistance. And together, we felled my mighty, arrogant brother. The only problem was that he had actually been smart in hiding you with your bloodstone. Part of its enchantment was a strange sort of protection. We couldn't return you to the Spiritlands ourselves to dispose of you and we couldn't permanently dispose of you in mortal form, because your soul was simply reborn time and time again. The only way for you to return to the Spiritlands was to do it on your own volition.

"That was the loop hole. The Fates decided that the best possible way of preventing your interference was to keep you mortal. So, Lachesis concocted the whole Keeper of Fate scheme. They captured Annen and Ahmose and forced them to work with them, to keep you in mortal form doing their bidding and out of our hair. And I can tell you, they had much fun at your expense making you punish your own parents time and time again."

My head snapped up. "My parents. Why were they there? Zeus and Cadmus didn't discuss that."

Hades waved a hand. "Oh, you know your mother. Once she heard of the plan, she wouldn't hear of it continuing without her. She wanted to be there, too. So, Zeus cast you all mortal."

"My parents knew, also?" I breathed. And for a split second, I saw satisfaction on Hades' face. And then it was gone, replaced by sympathy once more.

"Yes," he answered. "They both knew and they lied to you also. Now, I'll admit. Once they were mortal, they didn't remember anything. That was part of Zeus' plan. He was afraid that if he left you with your memories, you would all grow weary of waiting and return too soon, which would jeopardize his entire grand scheme. Your parents thought they were mortal nothings. And that played right into the Fates' hands."

"And yours," I snapped. "You are not innocent!"

"And mine," he agreed easily. "But I did not wish to harm you. I simply wanted you to stay away from the Spiritlands. I would have enjoyed having you here instead. But you're missing the point, sweet Harmonia. Everyone close to you lied to you. Cadmus, Aphrodite, Ares, Hecate."

"Hecate!" I exclaimed. "I completely forgot about her. How did she betray us?"

He smiled and this time, there was danger in it. He was a dangerous, dangerous man.

"Ah, Hecate. She did not do it willingly. Parents will do almost anything for their children. Her daughter was threatened and Hecate was told that if she complied with the Fates, her daughter would be released. But that wasn't their decision to make."

"I didn't realize that she had a daughter. Where is she?" I asked.

"Here," he replied.

I shook my head as my shoulders slumped. "So, they threatened her. Is there nothing good in the world? Is it all lies and deceit?"

"Perhaps so," he answered. "But the key is in finding beauty in the midst of ugliness. And you are that, Harmonia. You are beauty in a complex, vast sea of black."

He moved to embrace me and for one moment, I allowed it. I didn't trust him, but with the heavy knowledge that everyone around me had betrayed me, I just wanted to feel the comfort of someone. Anyone. For just a minute.

And in that scant minute, while I allowed the god of the Underworld to wrap his arms around me, Cadmus stepped onto the terrace with Ares and Persephone right behind me.

"What the hell is going on here?" His dark eyes snapped and he moved quickly to shove Hades away from me.

"Stop!" I screeched, throwing myself at him, pummeling his rock hard chest with my fists. "How could you? Cadmus, I trusted you. Out of everyone in the world, I trusted you. And you have betrayed me more than anyone else ever could."

He stood still and watched me in shock as he tried to make sense of what I was saying.

"I don't know what you mean," he answered uncertainly. "What did I do?"

"You don't even know?" I shrieked. "You have ruined everything and you can't even remember it. I will never trust you again."

"Hades," Persephone began, looking from her husband to me. "What is going on?"

"Ah, my love. Poor Harmonia has just discovered that she cannot trust anyone around her. They have all betrayed her. Isn't that horrible?"

Persephone was puzzled and turned to Ares. "What did you do?"

"Nothing!" he thundered. "You are lying!" He grabbed Hades and even without his powers, he threw Hades into the wall. Hades straightened and smoothed his clothing calmly.

"I assure you it is true. She saw it for herself."

"Then I want to see also," Cadmus interrupted. "*Now.* Show me what I did."

"Then drink," Hades waved toward the fountain. "Both of you."

Ares and Cadmus strode toward the fountain with matching steps and quickly scooped water into their mouths with their hands. I numbly waited. I was still so dumbfounded that I couldn't think. What was I supposed to do now that I couldn't trust anyone?

After a moment, Cadmus turned to me, his face filled with pain.

"Harmonia, I had no choice. Surely you can see that. Zeus gave me no alternative."

For once Ares remained silent. He knew there was nothing to say.

I watched my husband, the man who I knew every inch of, every thought, every dream…and I couldn't think past the pain of betrayal. It felt as though my entire world had shattered. Because if there was no trust, then what was there at all?

"Cadmus, you purposely kept it from me. You lied. I had no choice or say in it at all. And your lies are why I can't forgive you."

Hot tears streaked down my cheeks and blurred my vision. Cadmus rushed to soothe me, but I pushed him away.

"No. Don't touch me."

"You honestly can't forgive me?" The pain in his gaze gave me pause and ripped my heart out, but I couldn't lie. "You honestly can't understand the position that I was in?"

"I don't know. I've always trusted you as no other and you have destroyed that. I don't know if it is fixable. If only you hadn't chosen to lie to me… then, perhaps. But now…" My voice cracked with pain and trailed off. I struggled to avoid weeping.

"But Harmonia, can you not see that he was pushed into a corner by Zeus?" Ares interjected, his dark gaze thoughtful. "Surely you know that he would never knowingly hurt you. You know that."

"And you." My voice turned to ice. "You and mother lied to me as well. You all treated me like I was a child- too simple to make up my own mind or know the truth."

"It wasn't like that," Ares protested, holding up his large hands. "Harmonia, we were not given a choice either. You know Zeus. He had already made up his mind."

"But you didn't have to lie," I answered quietly. "None of you did. But each of you did it anyway. You betrayed me. I can't be with you right now."

I turned my back on them and struggled to maintain my composure. Tears dripped down my face and it didn't matter to me that I was standing in Hades' palace in the Underworld. The visions that I had on the hillside on the Necromanteion came rushing back to me. *Betrayed.* And I had thought it was Hecate and that was devastating enough. But instead, it had been everyone that I loved.

"I need to be alone for awhile," I mumbled quietly. Persephone wrapped an arm around my waist.

"Of course," she answered. "I'm sorry, Harmonia. I really am. I'll show you to a bedroom and you can rest."

I nodded. "Not the same bedroom as Aphrodite," I warned. "I need time alone to think."

"Absolutely," she answered and I allowed her to lead me from the room.

As we turned the corner, I glanced back. Cadmus looked shattered. His broad shoulders were slumped and he hung his head. He looked up and met my gaze and I could have drowned in the pain that I found in his eyes. But it didn't change what he had done.

As a goddess who had always been surrounded by the politics and back-stabbing of Olympus, I needed to know that I could trust my husband to always tell me the truth, to always be on my side. I suddenly felt more alone than I had ever been.

* * *

It was dark when I opened my eyes. I glanced around quickly. I was in a lavish bedchamber in the middle of a sea of silken bedclothes. Dark curtains had been drawn, blocking out the light. I took a minute to adjust to the darkness. My eyes were puffy since I had cried myself to sleep and I rubbed impatiently at them.

"You're awake."

A quiet voice came from the corner and I strained to see.

Hades was sitting in a chair, watching me.

"I brought you flowers from the gardens," he said quietly. "You seemed to enjoy them earlier. I thought you might like some in your room."

I glanced at the vase on the bed stand. The orange and pink blossoms filled the room with their rich fragrance.

"Thank you."

He nodded. "Of course. It is a small thing, but I thought it might make you happy."

"How long have I been sleeping?"

"Not long. A few hours. You needed to rest. And here in my home, you can replenish your energy. Have I mentioned how extraordinary you are? Simply being around you makes me feel peaceful."

"Well, I *am* the goddess of peace. Maybe that has something to do with it," I replied ruefully. "Is that why you were watching me sleep? You enjoy tranquility?"

He examined me for a moment, his dark gaze thoughtful.

"I enjoy peace at times," he answered slowly. "There is a time and place for everything."

He stood and approached the bed, sitting on the edge near me. "Harmonia, I am not what most people think that I am."

I raised an eyebrow as I tried to inconspicuously move away from him.

"Oh, really?"

He nodded.

"Really. It's true. Think about it, Harmonia. Are you what everyone thinks that you are? You are the Chosen One. Everyone thinks that you have a plan, that you have the knowledge and the power to put Zeus back into his rightful place. That you are confident and assured that every move you make is the right one. Is that the case?"

He studied me again. "Because I think it is not. I think you are a beautiful woman who has been forced into a position that she hates. So much pressure has been placed upon you and you have never asked for it. You don't know exactly what to do especially now that everyone around you has betrayed you." He picked up my hand. "Am I right?"

I swallowed hard. He had long fingers and they were curled around my own. And he was not wrong. I hated my position because I had no idea what to do.

"I thought so," he said with satisfaction. "So, see, lovely one? People are not what others sometimes think they are."

"If you are not the dark lord that people believe," I started tentatively. "Then, what are you?"

I couldn't help but study his face as he spoke. He was handsome in a very exquisite way. I knew I should be running as far away as I could from him, but I ached to be closer and that scared me. I dropped his hand and scooted across the bed.

He chuckled, but remained where he was.

"I know you feel it, too," he murmured. "But I'm patient. So I will wait. What am I, you ask?" He pondered that for a moment, running his long fingers up and down the length of the bed next to him idly as he thought.

"That is a very complex question. But here is a truth. There is no one person, god or mortal, who is all goodness and light or all darkness and shadows. Each of us is comprised of varying shades of gray."

"And what shade are you?" I asked tremulously. I felt my lower lip shake as I spoke. "Are you lighter shades or do you fall more toward black?"

He smiled. "I'm not a color wheel, Harmonia. Like anyone else, I'm comprised of a little bit of everything. I'm not a monster, I assure you. I'm just a man and I do what I need to do."

I snorted. "Just a man? You're a god. The god of the Underworld, no less. And the things that you 'need' to do are sometimes heinous, horrible things."

His dark eyes glittered and I felt as though he was impaling me with them. I felt like I couldn't move away from the pillows that I was propped upon.

"What about my brother?" he asked quietly. "Do you feel that Zeus is kind and gentle? He is not. He forced you into thousands of years of misery- simply to ensure that you would save him at a later date. He was willing to sacrifice you for himself."

"Not just for himself," I protested. "I don't like what he did, but I do understand that it was for the good of everyone in the SpiritLands. And I haven't been sacrificed. I'm not dead. I'm still here, alive and well."

Hades shook his head slowly, as if he was lamenting the fact that I was an innocent child.

"Are you well? You're cowering in one of my guest chambers in the dark and your beautiful eyes are red from crying. Harmonia, you don't always need to be so good and kind. Just once, you can curse him for doing this to you. It's alright. No one will hear you but me."

I met his gaze and lifted my chin.

"Yes, sometimes I feel like cursing and screaming. But it won't do any good. This situation is what it is. And I don't actually understand it, to tell you the truth. What is your part in this? Why are you still so interested in me?"

"What a strange question, Chosen One." He moved closer to me and ran his fingers along my forearm, lightly circling my birthmark. "You are exquisite and kind and beautiful. And something about you is so very vulnerable. I have this unexplainable urge to protect you."

His black gaze caught mine and he moved his fingers to my face, rubbing his thumb lightly along my bottom lip. "Let me protect you, Harmonia. Please. You wouldn't have to fight anymore or carry the weight of the world on your shoulders. I would fight *for you.*"

Breath exhaled from my lips in a rush. Until he uttered those words, I didn't even realize how weary I was of all the pressure that had been placed upon me. It was truly exhausting. And I ached to simply hand it to Hades. He made it sound so easy. But a truth that *I* knew was that when something sounded so easy, it was never the right thing to do.

"I can't," I answered simply. "You're asking me to switch sides… to change from good to bad. I cannot do it."

He threw his head back and laughed a mirthless laugh. "From good to bad? Have you not listened to me at all? Zeus is not good and I am not bad. We are simply what we are… comprised of both good *and* bad. Both of us… we each simply have a different agenda. That is all."

"His agenda is better for me," I replied coolly. "His plan includes my husband, while yours is simply keeping me here in the Underworld with you. And speaking of my husband, where is he?"

His expression changed to one of neutral innocence, something that made me wary.

"He is here," he answered. "I'm keeping him from you for the time being, as you requested. You wanted some time alone to think and you shall have it. Don't forget that they all lied to you, darling."

"As if I could," I muttered. "Are they safe?"

His face clouded over for a minute, but he quickly masked his displeasure. "Of course. They are guests in my palace. No one shall get to them."

His answer made me uneasy. But why in the world wouldn't it? I was secluded in a darkened bedchamber with the god of the

Underworld trying to seduce me while I was at odds with my husband. I'd be crazy not to be worried.

# Chapter Seven

*Snip.*

I pictured a frayed ribbon connecting me with my mother, my father and my husband. It was old and tattered and coming apart, but was still woven between and around us all, tying us together with a unified bond.

*Snip.* An imaginary pair of scissors cut through it, the shiny blades separating my tattered bonds with the people I had loved the most.

*Snip.* The blades flashed once more and the ragged ribbons fell to pieces in the wind.

I shook my head, trying to shake away the disturbing thoughts. I still loved my family. Of course I did. It was just so incredibly hard to get past the lies. When I thought about all of the mortal lives we had lived together, all of the pain, all of the heartache… it killed me that they had all knowingly cast me into that without telling me.

It pierced my heart and I felt like I couldn't breathe. They were everything to me. But they weren't who I thought. The people that I thought I knew were always honest with me, because they loved me.

*They loved me.* That thought kept plaguing me despite my pain. And I knew they loved me still. Just as I loved them. I knew that Cadmus was probably beside himself, worrying about me, wondering what I was thinking or feeling. I gulped. What a hideous, distorted mess.

But there was still one bond that was undisturbed, still as pure as it ever was.

Raquel.

A vision of her sweet face filled my head. Her dark hair and jade green eyes, so like my own. I hadn't really even had a chance to get to know her, because the Fates had hid her from me for so long. But my heart knew her. And I wanted her back.

I dipped my hand into the Fountain of Truth, watching as the water poured through my fingers. I sat on the marble steps leading up to it, leaning against the cool stone. True to his promise, Hades had allowed me privacy for the last couple of days. He had prevented everyone from coming to see me, allowing me the utmost of quiet and solitude. He'd allowed me to simply linger in my rooms alone. No one bothered me.

My mind felt numb, like I couldn't really grasp the hurtful things that I had recently learned. I was well aware that it was my body's defense mechanism. Shock always did that to a person... enveloped them in a cocoon of decreased sensitivity to allow them to process their hurt. I was still trying and it wasn't coming easily. So today, I thought I would venture out to the Fountain to see if I could discover where in the Underworld Raquel was being kept.

I focused on her, on her sweet little face, as I dipped the cup into the bubbling water and drew it to my lips to drink. The cold water slipped fluidly down my throat and I took another drink, patiently waiting to see visions of my daughter.

But that is not what I saw.

Instead, I saw an intimate moment with Hecate and her lover, Mormo. I almost blushed as I realized what I was watching. They were entwined in twisted sheets, their arms wrapped around each other.

The story of Mormo and Hecate was an old one and certainly not one that I had ever given much thought to, since it wasn't my business. He had been her consort for a long time. Or I guess I should say, *it* had been her consort.

Mormo was androgynous in the way that only an immortal could be. He could morph from female to male at his will, although he typically chose the male form. He was a vampire-like spirit who had wandered time for ages and ages. For a reason that no one knew, he had been cursed by Zeus to drink the blood of mortal children in order to remain immortal. Hecate had fallen wildly in love with him and no one knew if he had managed to bewitch her of if she had truly just fallen for his charms.

He didn't remain consistently by her side, in fact, he only visited her every few years. He never remained in one place very long. He was a wanderer and no one knew that much about him except that he had been cursed to roam as a blood-drinker.

But since he was in my vision today, I had a rare glimpse at his elusive face. He was thin and pale, with dark hair and gray eyes. He wasn't strikingly handsome, but he had an air of something special about him, something compelling.

He whispered into Hecate's ear and she moved closer to him with a sigh.

"I hate it that you always leave," she murmured. "Why must you?"

He smiled and moved away, rolling from the bed and pulling on his clothing.

"Because I must," he answered. "I'll return."

And then he was gone and the vision changed.

Hecate was watching a little girl run through a beautiful garden. The girl had long, dark hair that streaked behind her as she ran and she turned laughingly to look at her mother. Her eyes were gray- the same shade as Mormo's and I realized with a start that I had seen them before.

I had dreamed of them not too long ago. She was the woman who had asked for my help.

"Empusa!" Hecate called, "We must go. We have things to do."

"But I want to stay here, Mama," Empusa answered. "It's happy here." And she was right- it was why I loved gardens myself. They always seemed happy and peaceful.

Hecate smiled lovingly at her. "My child, we'll come back. Come with me now."

She took her arm and they walked away and my vision distorted once again.

This time, Empusa was in a dark place filled with shadows. She was older and breathtakingly beautiful, just as she had been in my dream. Her skin was pale and shimmery as she moved through the dark.

She murmured softly to someone and my vision expanded to reveal another person in the shadows. A child. I gasped and my heart thundered.

Raquel.

Empusa reached out and snatched deep red berries from my daughter's hands.

"No!" she cried out. "You must never eat here. Promise me, little one."

Raquel nodded, her face smudged with dirt, making her jade green eyes all the more luminous.

"Okay," she replied tremulously. "But I'm so hungry. I've been here so long. I don't like it here, Em."

"I know," Empusa answered. "We just have to hide a little longer."

She reached out to brush Raquel's hair out of her face before turning to me, locking her gray gaze with my own.

"Hurry," she implored. My breath caught on my lips.

"Harmonia, what in the world are you doing out here?"

The startled voice came from behind me and my vision turned black. I turned to find Persephone emerging from the palace onto the terrace, obviously surprised to find me outside.

"Why are you drinking from the fountain?" she asked curiously. "What did you see?"

"I saw my daughter," I answered shakily. "With Hecate's daughter. Do you know anything about this? Do you know where they are?"

She watched me with sympathy as she approached.

"There are many, many things that I do not know," she told me. "Hades does not share everything with me, unlike the bond that you and Cadmus share. I love Hades with every breath that I take, but our love is different from yours. You love only each other. Hades and I… we're different."

"Why should that concern me?" I stared into her eyes. "I do not care about your relationship."

"You should," she replied. "Because it will affect you today."

"How so?" I asked curiously, noting for the first time that she carried something partially hidden in her skirt. "What are you holding?"

"I was on my way to your rooms," she explained. "I have something for you."

"Why would you want to help me?" I asked, slightly suspicious.

"Because…I do not want you here," she explained simply. "I have nothing against you personally, my dear. But Hades is entirely too infatuated with you. You must leave."

I stared at her in shock. Before I could speak, she laughed.

"You thought I didn't know? Of course I knew. I know my husband like the back of my own hand. He has desired you for a very long time- before he had even set eyes on you. But Hades… well, when he desires things, it is simply to keep them. Just like an art collection. He enjoys surrounding himself with things that he considers lovely. It is me he loves, however, even if he samples other things of beauty from time to time."

I suddenly saw Persephone for what she was. A woman in love with her husband, even despite of his faults.

"So, how are you planning to help me?"

She lifted her hand and in it, she held Hades' Helm of Darkness. I gasped and she smiled a thin smile.

"I know. He will kill me when he finds out. Well, not literally. Please don't use it against him. He is… not what you think. He's vulnerable on the inside and he can be kind. I do not wish him harmed. Please, only use it for what you need."

I nodded slowly, reaching out trembling fingers to take it from her. It appeared as a simple warrior's helmet, made from bronze. But I knew of its powers. It was far from simple.

"Now," she said briskly. "You need to leave. Your family needs your help."

I looked at her questioningly. "My family?"

She nodded, looking over her shoulder. "Your parents and your husband are in the dungeons. Hades is keeping them there, but I know that he intends to transfer them to the Dungeon of the Damned, so you must hurry."

"Why would he do that?" I cried. "They haven't done anything to deserve damnation!"

She nodded sadly. "I agree. But sometimes, a reason is not needed here. Your parents are good people, Harmonia. And your husband loves you with all of his heart. I know that you do not want them harmed, even if you are angry with them right now."

"You're right," I agreed. "I would never want them harmed. How do I get to them?"

"The helm will render you invisible," she answered. "You will be able to slip in and free them, but getting out with be a trick. There is a hidden corridor behind the forging fires. If you can get to it, you can escape. Here is the key."

She handed me a large brass key, which I clutched tightly in my hand. "Use care, Harmonia. Hades will hunt for you for all of eternity."

The thought sent chills down my spine.

"What are you waiting for?" she nudged me. "Go. You must be quick."

I took off running, slipping the helmet on as I ran. Interesting enough, my hands and arms faded away and I realized that I was, indeed, invisible. No one could see me. As I picked up speed, I realized one other thing. I was running immortally fast. The helmet was blocking the limitations of the Underworld- my goddess abilities were back. I sighed a breath of relief as I blurred down the hallway in a streak toward the basement.

I made good time. I was standing outside of the massive iron doors within minutes. Cautiously, I slipped inside. It was like a different world in the dungeons as opposed to the beauty of the palace above.

It was dark, with the only light coming from wide-spaced torches on the walls. It smelled musty and dank and the walls were covered in condensation. Low moans echoed throughout the halls and I was instantly filled with trepidation. What had Hades done to my family? They weren't able to defend themselves… they didn't have their abilities here.

As I walked, my heart sank. The dungeons were composed of a labyrinth of halls and corridors. Each corridor was lined with musty cells, with prisoners of every type contained within. But as I searched, I realized something. My thoughts were being invaded by the sound of the prisoner's thoughts.

Because I was wearing the helm and my goddess abilities had returned, I was able to once again read thoughts. Obviously, I could block them out if I chose, but instead, I focused in and tried to hear Cadmus, Aphrodite or Ares.

For a while, all I could hear was the sad, depressing thoughts of prisoners. I kept looking in each cell as I ran, trying to find a familiar face. But then my name stuck out and I honed in.

Cadmus.

He was thinking of me. He was picturing me, and through his thoughts, I could see what I looked like as I had left with Persephone. I looked fragile and heartbroken- exactly what I had felt like. He had no way of knowing that I felt stronger now and he was devastated at my rejection of him.

My heart twinged and I desperately wished that I could forgive and forget everything that had happened. I loved him with every ounce of my being. I couldn't imagine my life without him, yet I couldn't make my heart forgive him, either. Shaking that thought from my mind, I focused harder, following the thoughts as they grew louder and I knew I was close to him.

Turning a final corner, the room opened into a large, dark room. Hanging from the walls, guarded by two hideous guards, was my family.

It was clear that they had been beaten. Aphrodite had blood streaking from her temple, dripping onto her clothing. Her eyes were closed as she hung limply from her wrists. Her fingers were turning blue from lack of circulation.

Ares' eyes were wide open and furious. He also hung from manacles and he was a bloody mess. He was covered in bruises and welts and it was obvious to me that he had resisted and they had beaten him all the more for it. Cadmus was the same.

My husband was covered in blood. And I felt certain that he had fought as much as he could to escape so that he could get to me. I could see the blood seeping from his wrists around the steel manacles where he had tried to work them loose. My eyes filled with tears. They might have lied to me, but I loved them. And this was no place for them.

Turning, I appraised the guards. They had the gray, ashen skin of the undead. And I regretted the decision that we had made to leave Zeus' sword with Ahmose for safekeeping. For the crime of hurting my loved ones, I would like to kill these guards, bring them back and kill them over and over until I felt like justice had been served.

But once would have to do.

I quietly lifted a heavy sword from a bracket on the wall and in one deft blow, I impaled them both. Both Ares and Cadmus snapped up their heads, straining to see what had happened.

"It's me," I called out as I approached. "I'm wearing the helm." I took it off as I stood in front of them.

Ares face erupted into a grin. "Harmonia! Thank the gods! Get your mother down first, would you?"

Obediently, I raced to Aphrodite's side and crushed her manacles in my grip, catching her as she slipped down the wall. She barely opened her eyes, in fact, one of them was nearly swollen closed. Anger boiled up from deep within. This atrocity would be avenged.

I laid her gently on the ground while I freed my father and Cadmus. As I broke Cadmus' locks, he embraced me gently, even though I knew it must hurt him. His arms were covered in bruises and blood.

"Please forgive me, Harmonia. I love you." His gaze implored me. "This is killing me."

My heart cracked.

"I love you, too," I murmured. "And I want to forgive you. I'm trying."

He dropped his head. "That's all I can ask, I suppose."

I gazed around the room. "Where are Ortrera and her warriors?"

Ares motioned toward an adjoining room. "In there. Come help me?"

We flew into the next room and found my sister and her small army waiting. They were no worse for the wear than the others, but they tried hard to conceal their pain. It was simply in their nature. I grimaced for her, however, when Ortrera took a step and her ankle cracked. It sounded as if it had been broken. I handed her the helm.

"Here. Put this on. It will allow your goddess abilities to return while you wear it- and your foot can heal so that you can walk. You should all take turns wearing it- but Aphrodite gets it next."

Everyone nodded their agreement.

"We must hurry," I told them as I glanced nervously over my shoulder. "Hades is planning on moving you to the Dungeon of the Damned, although I don't know when. It could be any time."

Ortrera healed in record time and was able to walk again within a few minutes. We crept down the corridor in search of the forging fires that Persephone had spoke of. And it didn't take long to find them.

They were enormous and took up one entire massive room. Workers shoveled iron into the fire to heat it and then laid the pieces on a huge stone slab to form them into various shapes with hammers. The sound was deafening.

There was an entire room of workers and we had only one helmet. We looked at each other and at the same time, Ortrera and I said, "Ares."

He nodded and took the helm from her, putting it on and instantly was rendered invisible. We scarcely had time to think before the entire room of workers were lying dead on the floor and Ares was once again standing in front of us.

"Let's go, then," he said nonchalantly as he motioned us toward the hall leading behind the fires. It led to another set of heavy doors, which I unlocked with the brass key that Persephone had given me.

No one questioned why I had it or how I had come to get it. Instead, the entire group remained silent as we raced through the passage that would lead us to freedom.

# Chapter Eight

As soon as we burst from the darkened corridor to the outside, I drew in a deep breath and looked around. Almost instantly, a cloud of red butterflies descended upon us.

"Thanks, Ahmose," I whispered. I knew that he was somehow watching us and helping us in what limited ways that he could.

"Where should we go?" Aphrodite asked. Ares was carrying her, although since she was wearing the helm, she was invisible.

I looked ahead of us and saw the thousands of heads of the undead army guarding the palace.

"Not that way," I muttered quickly. We spun around and circled around the palace and continued on behind it.

"We cannot stop right now," Ares stated calmly. "I wish that we could stop long enough to allow everyone to heal, but we cannot. Hades will deploy an army to find us as soon as he discovers that we are gone."

I nodded in agreement. "He will stop at nothing to find us. I know that much to be true."

We walked quickly forward. The terrain was easy, flat plains and low hills. The ground was soft under our feet.

"I should tell you..." I began and glanced around at the others. They stopped and waited for me to finish speaking. "I should tell you what I know."

Ares nodded. "Then speak, daughter. Although know this, when we have a moment, you and I are going to have a discussion."

I ignored the last part of his statement and continued. "I think that Raquel is in Tartara. I saw a vision- she was with Hecate's daughter, Empusa. It looks as though Empusa is helping her, but I can't be sure. They were surrounded by shadows and darkness... which leads me to believe that they are in Tartara."

Cadmus clenched his jaw. "Then we shall go, as well."

He reached out and grabbed my hand. I enjoyed the warmth of his strong fingers wrapped around my own for just a minute before I pulled away. I so wanted everything to go back to the way it was. But I couldn't forget the lies. It prevented me from forgiving him. Even though I wanted to.

He sighed, but remained at my side, leaning in to whisper in my ear.

"I'll wait for you, my love. Forever, if I have to."

I nodded, my eyes filling with tears. He gazed at me, his expression sad. He reached out and wiped my tears away.

"Don't cry, Harmonia. Everything will be alright."

"Will it?" I asked, my voice small and shaking. I wasn't so sure.

"Of course it will," Ares interrupted. "We'll talk more of it later."

I had to smile, just a little. Ares was so arrogant, which was one of the traits that I loved about him. Did he truly think that everything would be fine simply because he decreed it so?

"So, we go to Tartara," Aphrodite said. "We should move. I feel much better now. Someone else can wear the helm." She passed it to Cadmus. He tried to give it to one of Ortrera's warriors, but true to her nature, she insisted that he take it first.

"I'm fine," the muscled Amazon insisted. "You should go first." Her legs shook with exhaustion and pain, so it was evident that she was not 'fine', but she would never admit that.

Cadmus tried arguing with her for a few minutes before he realized that it was useless and he plunked the helm onto his head in resignation. As I looked at his chiseled face staring from under the visor, I had visions of watching him spar and fight in Egypt so long ago. My husband had always been a warrior.

It was strange. I was the goddess of peace, yet the two men I loved more than anyone in the world, my husband and my father, were warriors. And that was a fact that would come in handy in Tartara, I was certain.

I had never been there, but I had heard stories. Tartara was the place where the damned were sent, the heinous souls. It was guarded by the Erinyes and contained the Dungeon of the Damned, where the most hideous of prisoners were punished for all of eternity. It was said to be dark and desolate and it killed me to think that my daughter might be there.

"We need to go," I breathed, quickly turning and walking quickly toward the horizon.

"How do you know that you're going the right way?" Aphrodite called. I pointed upward at the cloud of butterflies that was lingering over my head directly in front of me.

"I think Ahmose is leading the way," I answered. If someone had told me even last week that I would be following a swarm of butterflies to the gates of hell, I would have thought they were crazy. But here I was.

Once again, we walked for hours. As we hiked onward, we felt fairly certain that we were going the right way because the sky darkened up as we continued.

The Amazons rotated the helm throughout their numbers until everyone had healed up and then Aphrodite and I passed it back and forth as our strength waned. I actually started to wonder if this was the very reason why Rhadamanthus had told us to acquire it in the first place. He had probably known, just as Ahmose had, what effects the Underworld would have on the two of us.

My legs were feeling overwhelmingly weary when I noticed a glow to the sky in the horizon, right where the sky met the land. As we continued on and drew closer, I realized that it was fire, a long line of it. I studied it curiously, but couldn't make heads or tails of it until we were upon it. And then I realized what it was.

It was the river Phlegethon… or otherwise known as the River of Fire.

I glanced down both lengths of it and it seemed to stretch on forever. It was wide, far too wide to leap across, even wearing the helm. The orange flames lapped up from the surface, grabbing at the fresh air that fed it. I could feel the heat from the fire from here and I couldn't see any way that we would be able to get through the flames to Tartara's gates.

My shoulders slumped and I sat abruptly on the ground, staring at the flames in desolation. I was so, so tired. Too tired to even begin to think of a good plan. Before I had even realized it, Cadmus sat next to me and pulled me into his lap. I began to squirm away, but he held me fast.

"Don't," he suggested. "Just let me hold you. It doesn't mean that you've forgiven me. It only means that you're still my wife and you're allowing me to comfort you."

He was right and I knew it. No matter what, no matter how hurt I was, he was my husband and I loved him more than anything. I leaned my head against his strong chest. He smelled like a man, like sweat and his familiar outdoorsy scent. I inhaled it as I closed my eyes. He stroked my back and allowed me to sit in silence for a few minutes. I heard the others discussing the river and how to cross it, but I didn't even open my eyes.

Instead, I silently cried. The stress, the drama and the emotion from the past couple of days welled up in me and I couldn't control it. The tears began flowing. As they did, my wrist started throbbing. The outline of my birthmark began glowing and I startled, gripping it, although it didn't hurt.

"What is happening?" I murmured through my tears. Cadmus snatched up my wrist and examined it, but before he could say anything, Ortrera shouted.

"Look!"

I followed her finger and gasped as the Phoenix descended upon us. It was massive and majestic as it swooped low over the river. The flames from the river leapt up and bled into the flames of the Phoenix. Its eyes were glowing and blue and they were fixated on me. I suddenly knew that I had somehow called it.

It landed a short distance away from us and stood quietly, its large wings quivering every so often. It was bigger than I remembered, as large as a small horse. Just as I remembered, it was made from flame, with brilliant blue eyes. As it burned, it studied me and I felt compelled to get up and walk toward it.

I stood in front of it and it dipped low, as if bowing to me. I shook my head.

"You don't need to bow to me," I murmured.

It remained in position and I looked uncertainly at the others.

"What do you think it wants?" I could feel the fire from its wings heating my cheeks and Cadmus grasped my hand.

"I think it wants you to climb onto its back," he said quietly.

"But I'll get burned," I protested, staring once again at the bird. One azure eye looked up at me. It did certainly seem like it wanted me to crawl onto its back. I took a shaky step.

"Remember the pit on Calypso's island?" my mother questioned me. "After the Phoenix appeared and you stepped into the fire, you didn't get burned."

The phoenix bowed even lower.

I caught a shaky breath and reached out to grip its neck. His fire did not burn me. Cadmus grabbed my waist and thrust me up onto its back and then quickly swung up behind me. I looked to him in alarm.

"As If I'd let you go alone," he admonished, raising his dark eyebrow. The light from the phoenix reflected off of his shiny, dark hair making it almost seem as if he was glowing.

"But you didn't know… you could've been burned. You didn't know if I was the only one immune or not…"

"It was of no matter," he replied firmly. "I would never let you go alone."

My chest filled with warmth. He was so brave and strong. And he loved me so much. I laid my hand on his sculpted thigh and twisted around to kiss his cheek.

I nodded silently, not trusting my voice as the Phoenix stood and then took off into the night. Cadmus held fast to me and I gripped the Phoenix' neck as we flew a wide arc above the river. Flames billowed around us but we didn't so much as singe a hair. As the Phoenix dropped gracefully to the ground on the other side, it bowed low once more to allow us to dismount.

Before I could even say anything, it was gone again. It returned quickly with Ares and Aphrodite on its back and then made several more trips for the Amazons. After everyone had joined us, the bird screamed into the night and took off. It had disappeared into the darkness before I could even blink.

"Well, that's that, then," Aphrodite murmured as she moved to my side. "That bird has come in handy more than once."

I nodded in agreement. "It certainly has. I just wish that I knew how I summon it. It always just seems to appear when it is needed."

She stared thoughtfully into the night sky. "I think you are connected to it. And perhaps that is the true nature of your birthmark. Perhaps it senses when you need it and it comes."

"Perhaps," I chewed my lip. "But that's neither here nor there now."

I glanced around us. This side of the river didn't look much different from the other side. But the entrance to Tartara loomed ahead of us. I could sense it more than I could actually see it. A bone-numbing cold emanated from that area and I shirked away as I stared into the dark.

It looked like an enormous cave with massive boulders on each side. I could hear wails coming from within and it sent chills up my spine. Near the entrance, there was a huge gray boulder to the left. The feeling of foreboding was almost overwhelming as I examined our situation. The heat from the river Phlegethon warmed my back and calves as I stood silent and still.

And then the breeze came from the south, rustling the hair on my shoulders and bringing with it a horrible, acrid odor…one I had certainly smelled before.

"Dragon," Cadmus said quietly.

We all peered closer into the night and found that the giant 'boulder' in front of the entrance was actually an enormous reptile. It appeared to be sleeping, but it was most certainly a dragon.

Its gray scales glistened in the light of the river and his massive tail, curled around its side, had sharp spikes lining it all the way to the tip. Large black claws curved into the ground, scratching every so often even in its sleep.

"I'm so sick of dragons," I muttered. "Seriously, just once, could we do something without encountering one?"

"It doesn't look that way," Cadmus said, turning to me with a confident grin. "But you're in luck. I'm a dragon specialist."

He held his hand out for the Helm of Darkness.

"Aphrodite, may I?" he asked.

"Of course," she replied quickly, snatching it off and handing it to him. "Just be careful."

He rolled his eyes and gestured toward the dragon's back leg. "This one is chained. It will be child's play. He is used to keeping people in, not keeping people out. He won't be expecting me."

"And why would he?" I muttered. "Normal people aren't clamoring to get into the bowels of hell."

With one last cocky grin, Cadmus pulled the helmet onto his head and he was gone. I could no longer see him.

We all held our breath as we watched the dragon and we knew the exact moment when he heard Cadmus approach. He lifted his massive head and stared into the night, his breath exhaling from his nose like steam. He looked one way, then the other and then forward in puzzlement. It was almost comical.

And then he lurched to his feet, throwing his head back with a scream. Blood dripped from his neck in thick, black streams. Cadmus had made contact.

The enormous reptile whirled around, screeching loudly as it searched for its attacker. But of course it couldn't see anything. Cadmus was invisible.

It spun around again, its tail whirling like a whip. It was so heavy that every time it moved, the ground shook around us. It reared up on its hind legs, the heavy chain that confined it rattling loudly before it crashed back to the ground, its eyes rolling wildly.

It was the strangest thing. We could not see Cadmus, we could only see evidence of the unseen battle in the wounds that were appearing on the dragon. A long, thin line of blood appeared on its side. Another wound.

Then it screamed once more, throwing its head this way and that, another gaping hole evident in the side of its neck. Black blood gushed and its giant head dropped to the ground, its massive sides heaving as it attempted to draw in air.

Its attempts were short-lived. It wasn't long before its chest shuddered to a stop and it stopped breathing.

And I started again. Inhaling deeply, I searched the night for my husband. I didn't see him and I fought panic. Where was he?

I scanned the darkness again, and he came into focus as he limped up to us, pulling off the helmet. Blood had drenched his clothes, and not the black blood of the dragon. His clothing was drenched with red blood... his own.

I gasped and rushed to him and as I got closer I saw the sharp leathery spike in his shoulder.

"From its tail," Cadmus explained with his jaw clenched tightly. "The beast got me by accident as it spun around."

Ares pushed past me and ripped Cadmus' shirt off, leaning close to examine the wound. My husband's blood pulsed around the base of the spike and Ares wadded up the ripped shirt and pressed it around the gaping hole.

"We need the witch," he muttered. "Of all of the times for her to turn traitor..."

"What do you mean?" I asked in alarm. "Just put the helm back on him. He'll heal."

Ares shook his head. "Daughter, you know that dragons have their own magic. We need special magic of our own to combat that. And I don't know any, do you?"

He glowered up at me as he hovered above my husband and I silently shook my head. He knew that I didn't. My breath exhaled in short pants.

"Then what should we do?"

"I'll be fine," Cadmus insisted, but he was grinding his teeth together from the pain. I rushed to him, clutching his arm.

"Don't die," I pleaded with him. "Please, don't die. We'll figure out something."

He gazed down at me, his dark eyes reflecting the fire of the river, his jaw clenched with pain.

"You care, then?" he asked softly. "If I live or die?"

"Of course I care!" I replied angrily. "How could you even ask that? I'm angry with you, but I'll never stop loving you."

He reached up with a bloody hand and stroked the side of my cheek. As he moved, the rusty scent of blood filled my nose and my cheek was sticky where he had touched. My heart raced. I couldn't let him die.

"Zeus," I breathed. "We must find Zeus- he can heal Cadmus."

"We must also find our daughter before Hades does," Cadmus replied huskily. "I'm sure he will want to use her against us now, Harmonia. He must surely know that we are gone by now."

Realization settled upon me like a wet blanket. They were probably pursuing us even as we spoke.

"Yes," I agreed quickly. "I'm sure they are on their way. What do you suggest we do, Ares?"

My father pondered that, his forehead wrinkled as he kept his hands pressed to Cadmus' wound.

"We should continue our course," he finally said. "And let us begin with Tartara since we are already here."

"But what about Zeus?" I demanded. "We must find him to save Cadmus."

Ares shifted his gaze to me and his dark eyes were calm.

"Harmonia, we don't know where to begin. We are already here, so this is where we should start. And there is one thing that you are forgetting. Zeus' sword. It can take away life, but it can also give it back."

I stared into his serious face. He thought Cadmus was going to die before we could even reach Zeus. I put a hand to my chest and took a deep breath.

Ares continued quietly. "We're as mortals right now, daughter. No mortal could survive that. He's losing too much blood."

I looked at my husband. Ortrera and Aphrodite had helped him to the ground and his eyes were closed. His bronzed skin was turning pale already from loss of blood.

I dropped to my knees next to him, clasping his hand.

"Cadmus," I murmured. "Open your eyes."

His chocolate eyes fluttered open, framed in a fringe of long lashes. By the gods, he was beautiful, even now. I brushed his hair out of his eyes and he leaned into my hand.

"Don't die," I instructed. "Stay awake, Cadmus. We'll find Zeus. He'll save you, but you must fight until we find him. Do you hear me?"

"Do you forgive me?" he whispered. "Can you forgive me for keeping the truth from you so long ago? If I could take it back and re-do it I would, I promise you." He coughed and I saw blood on the corner of his mouth. I swallowed hard as I wiped it away. "I can't die thinking that you can't forgive me, Harmonia."

"You can't die at all!" I cried. "Cadmus, please. I'm sorry. I know you didn't mean to hurt me. I forgive you- I do. But you cannot die."

He nodded weakly. "I'll try not to." He closed his eyes again and rested his head against my lap.

"It's alright, my sweet," I whispered, leaning down to kiss his forehead. "Rest now."

"We need to move," Ares said as he stared down at me.

"I know," I answered. "Why does this keep happening, Ares? Why? I've lost him in every life that I ever lived and even now, with the Fates gone, I'm going to lose him again."

"It's your bloodstone," he answered softly. "You know that it is cursed, Harmonia. Until the day that you no longer own it, misfortune will continue to follow you."

Anger exploded inside of me and I could barely think.

"Why in the hell did Zeus allow Hephaestus to curse it?" I demanded. "I understand the fact that he needed me to have it, that it has his blood in it…and I'm the Chosen One and all of that crap. But did he have to allow it to be cursed?"

Ares shrugged. "I know not, daughter. You know Zeus."

And that said everything right there. Zeus was not constrained or influenced by what might happen to others. He saw the big picture and he saw how things affected him and him alone. And suddenly, all of my anger that I had directed at my parents and Cadmus shifted to Zeus, where it belonged.

"You know, "I pondered angrily. "I have always held the Fates' responsible for my tragic lives, but perhaps it was Zeus all along. I'm sure the Fates enjoyed my tribulations and certainly, they deceived me into making your lives hell, too, but my own life—it would have been miserable no matter what. Because of Zeus!"

I spun around and stared at my mother. She looked at me helplessly.

"I don't know what you wish me to say," she answered. "You are probably right. But do not let the Fates off so easily. They used that very thing to their advantage and they *did* trick you for thousands of years."

"I know that," I muttered as I gently extracted myself from Cadmus' grip and stood up. "I do not need reminded. We should move now. There is no time to waste."

Ortrera was quietly instructing her warriors and they hurried to my side, kneeling around Cadmus. Making a make-shift gurney from their shields, they carefully lifted him to shoulder height.

He was shivering and I realized it was probably from blood-loss. I cringed at the realization and quickly dug through my knapsack for a wrap. I tucked it around my husband's body and kissed his soft lips before speaking to the group.

"Let's go to Hell," I said wryly, pushing forward without looking back. I felt the others follow me as I circled around the dead dragon and I paused only slightly in the entryway of Tartara.

I couldn't believe I was here. But I most certainly was and there was only one thing to do in order to get out. I had to enter. I took a step and then another and walked into Hell.

# Chapter Nine

Hell was dark.

As I picked my way over sharp rocks and through dry brambles and descended into the bowels of the Underworld, that was the thing that stuck out at me most. The absence of light. There were random fires here and there, which cast frightening shadows, but there was no other light here. It was black as pitch and freezing cold.

Ares strode forward to walk by my side at the front, his protective nature revealing itself. As we passed a small patch of brambles that were alight, he bent to pick up a long branch and lit it ablaze before holding it in front of us as a torch.

I wasn't sure that was better.

The fire illuminated our path, but it revealed everything else along the way. To our right, a blackened demon sat hunched over on a charred log. He smelled like sulfur and he had no eyes. As we walked past, he hissed loud and long, following our movements even though he couldn't see us. The pale blank areas where his eyes should have been sent shivers down my spine. Behind him, a long scaly tail twitched.

"Nice place," I mumbled to Ares as I scooted a little closer to him.

"Isn't it?" he replied somewhat cheerfully.

"Why doesn't this bother you?" I asked curiously. "It gives me chills, yet you don't seem fazed in the slightest." As I spoke, I glanced over my shoulder at the demon once again. He was still sitting motionlessly where he had been. Evil exuded from him and I couldn't walk fast enough in the opposite direction.

Ares glanced sideways at me for a moment before returning his attention to the terrain in front of us.

"Are you asking why Tartara doesn't scare me? It is because this place is nothing compared to the fear that I feel over losing anyone that I love. I have faced many things in my life and nothing is as terrifying as that. Perhaps it is because I do not love many people. I hold the ones that I do very close."

His muscles bulged as he moved, his shirtless torso glistening in the firelight. I hadn't even realized that he had taken his shirt off. Glancing behind us, I saw that it was tucked around the spike embedded in my husband's shoulder. The white linen cloth was soaked through with blood.

My eyes suddenly stung and I blinked hard.

Behind Cadmus and the Amazons, my mother and Ortrera were murmuring softly as they cast periodic glances into the darkness surrounding us. It was clear that everyone was on guard. Aphrodite caught my eye and gave me a comforting look, so I offered her a small smile in return before turning back around.

"Your mother is worried about you," Ares observed. "As am I."

"Thanks," I replied. "But it doesn't seem to be helping, so you should really save your energy."

He eyed me again, his dark eyes holding the kind expression of a father, not the god of war.

"I'm glad to see you still have your spunk," he finally answered. "So many others would lose that spark and grow discouraged after everything that you have faced. I'm very proud of you, Harmonia. You might not have been born to be a warrior like Ortrera, but you certainly inherited my grit."

"Not born to be a warrior!" I exclaimed. "Did you not just watch me kill two guards to free you from a dungeon?"

He laughed, his white teeth flashing in the dark. "Technically, no. I did not see you because you were wearing the helm. So, as far as I know, that could have been anyone."

I slugged him on the shoulder and he laughed again.

As we walked, I noticed a low moaning coming from somewhere, but I couldn't see where. After a few minutes, it grew louder and was accompanied by strange rasps and clicks. I peered into the darkness, but didn't see anything, yet the noise continued to grow louder with every step that we took.

And then, as we crested the top of a small hill, our view expanded and I froze, clutching Ares' arm.

We were facing an entire city-like civilization that seemed to be built from rubble. The sky above it glowed from the many bonfires and torches from within and the moans and wails creshendoed to an almost deafening roar.

My frightened gaze met that of my father's, although his was still unfazed.

"I think this is the City of the Sleepless," he stated calmly.

I stared at him silently, afraid to speak. It felt as though if I acknowledged what we were looking at with words, it would make it real. And I knew it was real. But if I didn't say it out loud, I could delude myself for a few minutes more.

But not long, because Ares continued.

"Dead souls in the Underworld do not sleep," he explained. "And just as sleeplessness can turn the living crazy, it can do the same to the dead. When a soul gives in to insanity here, they are brought to this city."

"You've got to be kidding me," I breathed. "An entire city of insane, sleepless souls?"

"I'm afraid he is not kidding," Aphrodite confirmed as she crept up behind me, laying her cool hand on my shoulder. "I've heard stories of this place, but I have never been unfortunate enough to see it for myself."

Until now.

We all stood on the crest of the hill overlooking this strange city of the insane, each of us lost in thoughts of our own. And then I took a step.

And then another and another, each step carrying me down the hill and toward the city.

The good news was that there was light. There were many, many fires and torches here and there, creating a bright glow. The bad news was that just like on the trail, the light revealed the terrifying things that surrounded us.

The Amazons set Cadmus down for a moment and reconfigured themselves. Only four carried Cadmus now, the other eight surrounded us in a protective, wary circle as we moved cautiously forward into the city.

Strangers walked, limped and crawled all around us. Most of them appeared haggard and dirty. But the oddest thing was that they looked alive. Their bodies were just as solid as mine. They were certainly not flitting about as spirits.

"Not what you expected?" Ares asked.

"Not at all," I replied. "I cannot tell the undead and the living apart, to tell you the truth."

He nodded in agreement. "It's true, it is difficult. And honestly, here in the Underworld, there aren't many differences between them and us."

I watched a pale, partially dressed man rummage through a trash-pile before I turned away. The thought of spending eternity in this dark place was depressing. I didn't even want to ponder what the man had done to deserve it.

I dropped back to walk next to my husband, although he was not awake. He slept fitfully, moaning softly every once in awhile and I knew that his wound pained him. That very thought pained me, too.

"We need to hurry," I urged Ares.

He called over his shoulder. "I know."

This city was unlike anything I had ever seen before. We stayed on the worn gravel road as we continued through the sad civilization. Barely anyone even glanced at us twice. Our presence was of no consequence to them. I doubted they even truly realized that we were there. Their minds were certainly gone.

To our left, a massive black pit teemed with writing pale bodies. Everyone was naked and they all screamed as they clawed at the sides. I inched closer to Cadmus. Everything about this horrible place was unnerving.

"Are you alright?" Aphrodite asked me gently.

"Yes. Are you?"

"I'm not sure. Ask me when we've left this place," she shuddered. "A more miserable place I've never seen."

Ares called back to me, interrupting our conversation.

"Harmonia? Can you come here?"

My mother and I exchanged quick puzzled looks before I made my way back to the front.

I found Ares staring in hesitation at someone in a small, secluded area. I followed his gaze. The woman was hooded, her dirty hair falling around her shadowy face. She was muttering incoherently with her legs sprawled in front of her, scratching into the ground with an old rusty piece of metal. She had written the same thing over and over in scraggly, thin writing.

*EMPUSA*
*EMPUSA*
*EMPUSA*
*EMPUSA*

My startled gaze flew to my father's.

"Isn't that Hecate's daughter's name?" he asked slowly. I nodded, taking one step in the woman's direction.

Ares grabbed my arm. "Wait! Let me."

He approached her slowly, the same as he would a frightened animal. The woman lurched to her feet and hunched away from him into the corner, whimpering.

"Don't, don't, don't, don't," she whispered.

He knelt in front of her, holding out one hand slowly.

"Hecate?" he asked.

"That's not Hecate," I shook my head. "There's no way, Ares."

He glanced up at me.

"Don't be so sure," he muttered, returning his attention to the dirty woman.

"Hecate?" he asked again, this time moving a little closer. She clasped her hands over her ears and began screaming. Her shrill shrieks filled the air and I resisted the urge to cover my own ears to block out the horrible sound.

He reached out a hand to touch her and she wrenched away. As she did, however, her hood fell down, revealing her face.

It was most certainly Hecate.

I froze, as did Ares.

"Hecate," I whispered, moving to touch her. She lurched to her feet and took off sprinting. She made it three steps before Ares had tackled her to the ground, holding her down as he tried to reason with her. Hecate seemed terrified, as if she had never seen us before in her life.

I loomed over Ares' shoulder.

"I'm not sure that man-handling her is the best way to get her to trust you," I remarked. "What do you think has happened to her?"

"I know not," he shook his head. "It is this place. It can turn the sanest person crazy."

As if on cue, Hecate began wailing about Empusa again in incoherent, desperate words.

I dropped to my knees next to her.

"Are you trying to find Empusa?" I asked quietly.

She stopped crying and stared at me with liquid, hazy eyes.

"Do you know her?"

Her question was crystal clear as she gazed into my eyes.

"It's complicated," I replied carefully.

"Ares," I turned back to him. "What can we do?" I was referring, of course, to Hecate's mind. She had lost it. And Ares knew exactly what I was talking about.

"I don't know," he replied limply, loosening his hold on the goddess of witchcraft. It was hard to believe at this current juncture that Hecate had recently summoned armies from the Underworld to aid us in Camelot. She was utterly helpless right now. "Try your bloodstone."

I pulled it over my head and pressed it to her skin. She looked at it fearfully, but didn't exhibit the normal awakening behavior. It had no effect on her and the hope fizzled out of me. This was the first time that the Bloodstone hadn't worked and I couldn't imagine why- unless Hecate was just too far gone or if maybe even her internal magic was just too strong- it was subconsciously blocking the Bloodstone.

"I wish that we had access to the Fountain of Truth," I muttered. "It would surely restore her memories."

"Harmonia," Aphrodite began hesitantly from my shoulder. I turned around quickly- I hadn't even known she had been standing there. I had been that focused on Hecate.

"*You* have drunk from the fountain- very recently. It is in your blood." Aphrodite's face was anxious and cautious as she made the unspoken suggestion. Her statement triggered a memory... of Lachesis drinking my blood in Camelot to expose the truth. She had wanted to see if I was lying and my blood had exposed that I was.

And then I remembered Hecate herself telling me that blood could reveal the truth. I sighed.

"Do you have any idea how tired I am of people drinking from my blood at this point? This is getting ridiculous," I complained. "At this rate, I'm not going to have any blood left soon." Regardless, I positioned myself closer to Hecate and pulled out a small dagger.

"Hold her tightly," I instructed my father. He complied and I cut a tiny slit in my arm, holding it above Hecate's lips. She didn't open her mouth, so my father forced it open.

"Gently," I snapped at him. "There's no need to be so rough."

"Besides the fact that she betrayed us all," he replied angrily. "I do not take to traitors kindly."

"She was coerced, I am sure of it. We need to keep that in mind," I pointed out as I dropped a few drops of my vital blood into her mouth. Ares held her mouth shut until he made certain that she had swallowed it and then we waited.

And waited.

And waited.

Her face was blank and impassive as she stared absently past us and I started to get panicky. What if she really was so far gone that nothing would work to bring her back? There were so many things that I wanted to talk to her about. I wanted to find out why exactly she had betrayed us and I needed to find out more about her daughter so that I could find my own.

But it appeared that I would get nothing from her. She stared right through me, her eyes flat and empty. The chilly air whipped around me as I turned to Ares dejectedly.

"It's of no use. Let her go."

My voice was stark and hopeless and I hated the sound. But it was how I felt. I had no idea what to do now.

"Harmonia?"

Hecate's murmur was so low that I had to strain my ears to hear it and I whipped back around, my heart thundering with hope.

"Hecate!"

She sank to the ground, hugging herself with shaking arms. Before I could say another word, she wilted further into the stones surrounding her and closed her eyes. She didn't reopen them. I shook her shoulder, trying hard to wake her, but she remained asleep.

I turned to my parents in exasperation. "Now what?"

Ares pivoted in a circle, examining our frightening surroundings and the appearance of our little group. Every one of us looked ragged and tired. Cadmus looked far worse. He was unconscious and shaking. I stroked his arm and rubbed his cold hands with my own. When I looked up, I found Ares staring at my husband in concern.

"We need to rest," he stated simply. And I didn't argue.

Ares hefted Hecate into his arms and we began walking once more, looking around for a safe, secluded place to stop for a few hours. We found a horse-shoe shaped inlet in the midst of a crumbling, abandoned building and quickly set up a makeshift camp.

We settled down to rest while half of the Amazons stood watch. Aphrodite crouched next to where I lay with Cadmus. She reached out and stroked my back.

"My sweet, everything will turn out alright. I have faith in that."

I couldn't meet her gaze.

"Will it?" I replied quietly. "We've been through so much, mother. Perhaps we're not meant to 'turn out alright.'"

She shook her head lightly. "I don't believe that," she replied. "You're a good person, Harmonia. You're a fighter and you have always chosen to do the right thing. I don't think that kind of behavior will be rewarded with tragedy."

"Yet, it has been already," I answered sadly. "Time and time again."

"But the end of that is near," she assured me. "I don't know how I know, but I just feel it."

"I hope you're right." But as I watched my wounded husband sleep, his face tightened with pain, all I could feel was discouraged. I didn't know how much longer Cadmus could hold on. If he died, this time it would be permanent, unlike all of the mortal lives that he lived and died in. Without Zeus, no one could bring him back. I fell asleep with his name on my lips and his limp arm wrapped around me.

It didn't take longs for dreams to consume me.

I was standing in knee-high purple flowers. Fields and fields of them, with billowing blue skies above me. A child's laughter distracted me and I turned, the sweet scent of the flowers assailing my senses. In addition to the floral notes, I detected salt in the air. Sea salt.

Raquel ran among the flowers, turning to laugh and yell over her shoulder.

"Come on, Em!"

"I'm coming." And I realized that Empusa was standing directly next to me. She leaned toward me, her gray eyes smoky and serious.

"Hurry," she murmured as she pressed a dark purple flower into my hand.

I awoke with a start, staring into my husband's eyes.

I startled, then gasped, as I realized that he was awake. As my eyes adjusted to the dark, I saw that Hecate was kneeling at his side, attending to his wound and I gasped again. She glanced up from her work with a small smile tilting the edges of her mouth. But before I could say anything to her, Cadmus slid a large hand into my own. As he did, I realized that I was holding a purple flower blossom.

# Chapter Ten

"You're awake!" I cried, throwing my arms carefully around his neck. He winced slightly, but pulled me close with his uninjured arm.

"Did you doubt?" he asked, one dark eyebrow raised. "Did you really think that you could get rid of me that easily?"

"That easily?" I repeated incredulously. "You were *this* close..." my voice trailed off and I didn't want to say the words. Instead, I kissed him gently and squeezed his hand, reveling in its warmth. He nodded, closing his eyes again wearily.

"I'm here now. And you've apparently found Hecate. Incredible... a guy can't take a quick nap without the entire game changing."

He tried to joke, but I wasn't in the mood at the moment. I had come perilously close to losing him. I could still scarcely believe that for once, I had not. I tightened my grip on the flower before turning my gaze to Hecate. I sat up as I spoke, keeping Cadmus' hand in my lap.

"Hecate, I'm glad you're feeling better."

"You can say it," she said without looking up, her fingers deftly moving over Cadmus' injury, sprinkling what appeared to be ashes. "You're glad I've regained my sanity."

"Yes," I admitted quietly. "You're right."

"And there is much you'd like to know," she prompted.

Once again, I agreed. "Yes. But first, I'd like to thank you for helping Cadmus."

She finally paused her moving hands and looked up at me. When she did, I could tell that she had been avoiding it because she had been afraid to see my expression. My heart twinged a little.

"You're welcome," she sighed. "It's the least I could do."

I stroked my husband's thumb with mine as I spoke. "What happened, Hecate? Why did you do it? Why did you betray us?"

She looked away as she tried not to cry, her beautiful blue eyes welling up with tears. Her angst was evident in her tortured expression and I had no doubt left in my heart that whatever she had done, she had been forced into it.

"The man that I love is not as loyal or admirable as Cadmus," she replied quietly as she began working over my husband once again. "But I can't help but love him anyway. It has been that way for many, many years. I give him the best of me and he gives little in return but his fleeting presence, once every few years.

"During one of his visits, I became pregnant with a daughter. And when she was born, I loved her more than any other thing on the face of the planet. She was all that was right and good in the world, even though her father was considerably less so."

She paused for a long moment as she bent to study the gash in Cadmus' shoulder. Pushing against it firmly, she pulled the dragon's spike loose and pressed herbs into the wound.

"What is that?" I questioned curiously.

"Oh, it's a medley of things, but it is comprised mostly of dried dragonheart blossoms… with a few other things of course." I didn't even bother asking what the 'other things' were. I was sure I didn't want to know.

"Most people would not know that dragonhearts can be used to combat the effects of an actual dragon's blood," she explained.

"I didn't even know that there were such things," I admitted, watching as she quickly sewed the wound together over the herbal compress.

She glanced up at me for a moment before continuing. "They only grow in a few secluded areas of the pacific rim in the mortal world. They are worth their weight in gold when someone has a dragon injury. Thank the heavens I thought to bring a few."

She gently finished wiping at Cadmus' shoulder. "That should do it. The herbs will be absorbed into Cadmus' bloodstream and then they'll dissipate on their own. I'll remove his stitches in a couple of weeks. I think he'll be fine."

"Thank you so much," I told her quietly as I stroked the side of his bronzed face. Leaning in, I kissed him again. "You'll be fine now," I murmured against his lips. He smiled without opening his eyes.

Straightening, I focused on Hecate again. "Go on," I prompted gently. "Tell me more about your daughter."

She sat back with her fingers to her lips, staring past me into the night.

"Empusa," she mused with an unreadable expression. Her face contained love, regret, sadness, despair and a haunting fragility. It was clear that whatever else, her daughter made this strong goddess vulnerable.

"It was her," I whispered. "They threatened her, didn't they?"

She looked away, blinking hard, before she continued.

"They made the offer, but it was her own father who accepted it. I'll never forgive him for that. I've loved him for thousands of years, overlooking his faults, but *this*...this I will never forget. Mormo was cursed by Zeus long ago. In order to stay immortal, he had to drink from the blood of children. He hated it at first, but then, I think that he actually began to like it. His soul began to turn ugly. He hated that his immortality was contingent on something. He hated that he *had* to do anything. So, when Hades made him the offer... that he could exchange his daughter for true immortality, Mormo accepted.

"I couldn't believe it. I was beyond devastated, but there wasn't anything I could do. The deal was made and no matter how powerful my magic was, it was useless against Hades. Empusa was sent to the Underworld and not only was she imprisoned here, but she was cursed to be as Mormo was. My sweet, innocent child has been forced to drink blood to remain alive. She will be forever frozen at just seventeen and if she stops drinking mortal blood, she will die."

Hecate's voice was almost a whisper at this point, painful and thin.

"That isn't the worst of it."

My head snapped up as I waited for her to explain what could possibly be worse.

"I found out later that everything was because of me. Hades didn't make the deal with Mormo because he liked Mormo or even because he truly wanted Empusa as one of his subjects. He made the deal because he needed leverage to use over me. He needed me to help overthrow the Olympians. He knew that Empusa was, and still is, the only thing that I would sacrifice anything for.

"He offered to reverse the bargain. He would send Mormo back to the Underworld and release my daughter if I helped him."

I watched her helplessly as tears streaked down her face and she dropped her slender hands limply into her lap.

"So I did."

She cried silently with her head bowed and I couldn't restrain myself anymore. Yes, she had betrayed us all. But she had been placed in the most unimaginable of positions and I found that I could not hate her for that. Not only that, but I was fairly certain that I would have done the same thing.

I unfolded myself from Cadmus' side and rushed to Hecate, wrapping my arms around her shoulders.

"Shhh, Hecate. It's alright. You have done what any mother would do. I would have done the same."

She stopped and looked up at me with watery, reddened eyes.

"Truly? I think not, Harmonia. You always have done the right thing. You would not have made such a mess."

"I make messes all of the time," I answered. "Look around you."

"This is not of your making, Harmonia," she sniffed. "We're here because of my magic. I enabled the Fates and Hades to trick Zeus. Everything is my fault. And I have not told you the last thing. I do not deserve your sympathy, I assure you. After you found Zeus' sword and I sheathed it for you, I offered incantations to try and roll back the Fates' manipulations… to try and undo their effects on my daughter. That very thing caused your daughter to be taken away. It's my fault."

I stilled for a moment. I wanted to scream and rail, but it wouldn't do any good. She hadn't meant any harm. She had only been trying to save her daughter- something that I should understand very well. After a few minutes of deep breathing, I was able to speak.

"It is alright, Hecate. I do understand. I do not hold it against you."

Confusion clouded my thoughts though, as I recalled my visions of Empusa.

"Hecate, I don't understand one thing. If you upheld the bargain, why is Empusa here? I've seen her in visions- she asks for my help. And I know that she is with Raquel."

Hecate froze, her gaze locked with mine. "Is she well?" she asked haltingly. "She has not appeared to me in quite some time. She doesn't trust me anymore."

"Why would she not trust you?" I asked uncertainly. "You have sacrificed everything for her."

"She doesn't trust anyone anymore," she replied sadly. "That is why she is still here. Once she heard what I had done, she went into hiding here. Hades decreed that she must appear in front of him so that he could lift the curse, but she is too afraid, so the bargain that I made was nullified. She has heard of your prophecy and because of it, she is terrified. She is afraid that Hades will kill her as a pawn. And she feels certain that once Zeus is restored, he will condemn me… and her, as well. So, she is afraid that either way, she will be killed.

"She hides in the bowels of the Underworld, afraid to come out."

A lump formed in my throat and I found it difficult to swallow.

"And what of Mormo?" I murmured hesitantly. "If Empusa is here, then is he still free?"

Hecate nodded slowly. "Since Em chose to stay here, Mormo is free to wander the mortal world at his will."

The breath expelled from my lungs with a rush. How utterly unfair.

"Hecate, we will fix this," I assured her. "Look!" I opened my hand, the purple flower shriveled on my palm.

"With a dead flower?" she asked dubiously.

"You doubt?" I asked. "Dead flowers healed Cadmus."

She shrugged. "I'll give you that, Chosen One. Tell me of this flower."

"Yes, tell us of this flower," Aphrodite interjected as she and Ares approached us from the shadows. "The story thus far has been fascinating, I will admit." Her tone didn't match her words. She was furious. I could tell from the tight way she was pressing her lips together.

I put out a hand.

"Mother, surely you can see how Hecate was coerced. She is a mother trying to protect her child. You of all people can understand that."

"Of course I can!" Aphrodite exclaimed indignantly. "If it is the truth. But Hecate has already betrayed us once. Why would she tell us the truth about it now? Anyone who can back up her story is imprisoned somewhere. She wants us on her side, daughter. She will tell us anything. And you are too trusting."

"I've spoken the truth," Hecate insisted. "I have nothing to gain from lying now."

"Nothing but gaining my sister's cooperation," Ortrera interrupted as she joined the group. "Aphrodite is right. Harmonia is too trusting by half."

"Thanks," I replied grumpily. "I am not too trusting. I choose to see good in people, as you should, too. I believe Hecate. I do. And I know that at least one thing is true. Empusa is definitely here in the Underworld. I've seen her in my visions. She has Raquel."

At our daughter's name, Cadmus opened his weary eyes.

"Where are they, wife? And is she safe with Empusa?"

"Of course she is safe!" Hecate replied quickly. "Empusa would never hurt her. She is probably trying to help."

"I do think that is correct," I answered calmly. "Empusa seems to be helping Raquel. She wants us to hurry and find them. She left this with me today." I showed them the flower. "They are somewhere surrounded by fields of purple flowers. And I could smell the sea in the air."

"I know of the place," Hecate broke in excitedly. "There are vast fields of flowers just like these near the oceans of Elyria."

Cadmus instantly opened his eyes and carefully sat up. Pulling off the wraps that had been placed around him, he stood. "Then we should go."

He was determined, even though I knew he was still in pain. He was a warrior. He had always been a warrior. And I should have expected no less from him. A near-death experience would never slow him down- especially when his daughter was on the line. He held out his hand, large and strong, and I took it, turning to my parents.

"I know that you might not trust Hecate right now. And that's understandable. But the fact is that her daughter is with mine—which means that we are traveling to the same place. Mother, can you put your reservations aside for now… for Raquel's sake?"

Aphrodite sighed. "You know that I will do anything to help you."

I stared at her for a moment. "And that is exactly my point. You would. And Hecate feels the same for Empusa. You should think on that."

I turned to Cadmus. "Are you sure that you are up to it? You're not completely healed. You still have stitches---"

He interrupted me firmly. "I'm ready." He looked around us curiously, examining our surroundings. I saw his gaze pass over the crumbling building that we were in, the partially decomposed walls and watched as he registered the horrid wailing that came from outside.

"Where are we?" he asked, his forehead wrinkled. "And what is that infernal racket?"

"You don't want to know," I muttered, rubbing his arm. "The important thing is that we're leaving here. And let us hope to never come back."

"I hate to bring up an unpopular idea," Ares mentioned, although his face didn't reflect any hesitation at all. "But since we are already here, I think we should pay a visit to the Dungeon of the Damned on our way out."

"And why would we do that?" Hecate demanded, her eyes snapping impatiently. "Empusa and Raquel are waiting. We must hurry."

I quickly filled her in on what Ahmose had told me about Alexi and Eris… and how we thought that we could somehow use Alecto to our advantage. She nodded thoughtfully as I finished.

"That is a very good point. And don't forget, we have allies here. Uther Pendragon is in Elysia, along with the other ancient chieftains. I'm sure they haven't forgotten that we helped Arthur put Camelot to rights. And we also have a few heroes scattered about. Achilles comes to mind. I'm sure he would help us and there are more."

"You're right," I agreed. "We certainly are not alone. On our way out, let's speak with Alecto and see where we stand with her. It is possible that once she finds out that Alexi's soul is in the Keres' box, she will work with us to bargain with the Keres. They have gotten what they wanted by imprisoning their sisters, the Fates, here. But perhaps they would further help us now."

"It can't hurt to talk with Alecto," Hecate replied. "And we won't lose much time. It is on our way."

We separated to pack up and within minutes, we were traveling once again.

Ares tossed the helm of darkness to Cadmus.

"You should wear that- it will heal up your wound. Glad to have you back."

I couldn't help but smile. There was a time, long ago, when my father and Cadmus hadn't gotten along so well. Cadmus had killed Ares' dragon without knowing who it belonged to and it had caused a huge ruckus in Olympus. As penance, Cadmus had been bound to Ares as a servant for eight years. It had turned out alright, even though it had been rocky at first. Cadmus and I had fallen in love and Ares had grown very fond of him. At that point, Ares' had granted permission for us to be married and the rest had been history.

I watched him conversing easily with Ares now and it warmed my heart. Family was important to me and I loved that we had such good relationships.

Our journey through Tartara was surprisingly uneventful. It was a frightening place to be sure, dark and shadowed. Misery hovered over our heads the entire way, but that was how it was meant to be. Nice people weren't relegated here, only the most heinous of souls.

We heard the Dungeon of the Damned long before we saw it. Screeches, wails and moaning echoed for miles down the trail leading up to an enormous stone wall. The wall was covered in moss and consisted of heavy cut stones. It was at least twenty feet high. There were wide wooden doors, but there was no guard on our side. There was no need. No one wanted to get into the Dungeon of the Damned.

We opened the doors and walked directly inside. To our right, there was a strange sort of courtyard filled with torturous looking devices. A screaming prisoner was being drawn and quartered by one of the Keres' sisters. I recognized her bleeding eyes. Their eyes continually bled from all of the things that they had seen. But this was interesting. It meant that they were here in the Dungeon assisting the Erinyes.

We slipped past the gruesome scene and around the corner, where we found a door to a stone and steel building. It was solid-there was no escaping it. With its foreboding atmosphere, it reminded me vaguely of the old prison, Alcatraz.

Ares didn't hesitate. He simply opened the door and walked in. Cadmus followed and the rest of us trailed behind.

It was hot as the blazes in the building, most likely from the many raging fires that burned within. The walls were scorchingly hot to the touch, so we had to ensure that we didn't lean on them. I learned that the hard way and I had a burn on my arm to show for it.

We wound our way through the dark corridors as we attempted to find the Erinyes. The wails were just beginning to cause a low ache behind my left eye when we finally turned a corner and stumbled into just the person we were searching for.

Alecto.

She was alabaster white, like so many were in the Underworld since they could never experience the warmth of the sun. Her hair was long and red and she wore tight black pants and a ruby red cloak. She turned her face toward us and I had to force myself not to show any outward signs of shock. Her eyes were pure black.

"Ares!" she exclaimed, her voice husky. I had to admit, she wasn't what I expected. I had expected something like the Keres or the Fates, stooped hags. She was not.

"What can I attribute this pleasure to?" she asked, her gaze sweeping over the rest of our group. "You seem to have brought an army."

"I'm sure you are aware of what is going on," Ares replied, not unkindly. "How you stay abreast of things in here, I do not know, but you always seem to."

She nodded slowly. "Yes, I am aware," she confirmed. "But that does not explain why you are here in my dungeon."

She stopped moving and stared into my father's face. Moving closer, she stood directly in front of him.

"The god of war is afraid," she murmured, reaching out to trace his face with her fingers. "You are afraid that you are facing insurmountable odds."

He stiffened and moved back a step.

"I am not afraid," he growled. "I am concerned." He turned to the rest of us. "The Erinyes have the ability to gauge one's fear. They can see what we are afraid of. That is a gift that is put to great use here."

I could see that. To our right, a man was in a small cell completely covered in writhing snakes. I assumed that his greatest fear involved the reptiles. And that made sense. The Dungeon of the Damned was even more formidable when it was your own personal hell.

"And you," Alecto turned to me. "You are afraid of loss."

"Yes," I confirmed. "I am afraid of losing those who I love."

"Your fears are valid," she nodded. "How can I help you, Chosen One?"

"We're not really certain," I admitted. "We only know that we will need friends while we are here. We don't know how things will go. But we do bring news of your son, Alexi."

Her head snapped up.

"What of Alexi?"

"His soul is in the Kere's box," I explained. "He is fine, he is being kept safe in the Spiritlands. But the Keres hold his soul."

She bellowed a horrendous screech.

"Thanatos!" she shrieked.

The Keres turned from where she was attending to a prisoner. Blood dripped from her hands.

"Yes?" she creaked.

"You have imprisoned my son's soul? Was this not something you felt you should share with me?"

Thanatos' expression relaxed. "I had forgotten, actually, with everything else that went on. Yes, we are holding Alexi's soul. He had fallen into league with our sisters."

"Give it to me," Alecto demanded.

"You know I cannot," Thanatos replied brusquely. "He must come before me so that I can merge it back with him. You know the way of it. Either that or he must stand in front of Hades." She shrugged.

A blue vein pulsed in Alecto's forehead, a clear sign of her displeasure.

"Fine." She turned back to us. "Bring him to me. Bring him to me and I will compensate you with valuable knowledge."

"What kind of knowledge?" I asked.

"I will share with you a portal out of the Underworld," she answered confidently. "Few know of it- it is a closely guarded secret. Anyone can enter from the outside, but only the pure of heart can use it to exit."

"If we accept the bargain, you will have to share the knowledge simply so we can leave to retrieve your son," I pointed out. "You will need to trust us to return."

"Oh, I know you will return," she answered. "Because I will want you to retrieve him now, before you continue on your quest."

I startled, then calmed myself. "That will not be possible. I must reach my own daughter. She's in grave danger."

Alecto showed no reaction. "Would you like to know of this portal?" she asked. "Would you like to secure my help in the future should you require it?"

"Of course I would," I answered calmly. "But not at the expense of my daughter."

She stared at me for a moment, her black eyes bottomless.

"There may be a compromise. I have Annen here. I will send him and you can send with him several of your Amazon warriors. Would that suit you?"

I turned to Ortrera with my eyebrows raised. She nodded at my silent question. I turned back around.

"Fine."

She summoned Annen and within minutes, the old man stood in front of us. He was identical to his brother, Ahmose, in almost every way. He had a shaved head, glittering dark eyes and long fingernails. Ancient writings lined his arms and a long black cloak swirled around his feet.

She explained his mission and he nodded obligingly. He was mute- he could not speak. The Fates had cut out his tongue. I eyed him warily. In another debacle with the Fates, he had burned words onto my hands to communicate. It hadn't been pleasant.

He motioned toward four of Ortrera's warriors. Once again, I turned to my sister and she nodded once. I motioned to Annen that it was alright.

"Annen can show you out," Alecto stated, already turning away from us. "I'll look forward to seeing my son."

And that was that. We were dismissed. We looked at each other uncertainly, but Ares moved toward the door.

"We have no time to waste," he muttered as he strode back down the long hall. "We must move."

And so we did. We made our way back through the Dungeon and were not hassled at the gates by the guard, since Annen was with us. We passed effortlessly from the Dungeon back out into the blackness of Tartara night.

I turned to Annen. "I feel like I should be angry with you, but I can't find the energy. You hid your identity and intentions from me for a very long time."

He looked at me with glittering eyes, but obviously didn't say anything. He couldn't. He shook his head, as if saying that I didn't understand. And I had to agree. I didn't. So, until I did, I would wait to judge.

I turned my attention to my husband instead. He had taken off the helm by now and appeared to be feeling much better.

"Do you feel better, my love?" I murmured, stroking the side of his arm. He nodded.

"Much," he answered. "Even more so now that we are moving toward our daughter. It won't be long now, Harmonia. I can feel it."

"I hope you're right," I answered. He slipped his arm behind my back and we continued on silently, each of us lost in our own thoughts.

Annen led us straight to the portal and surprisingly, it didn't take long. It was within the boundaries of Tartara and upon approach, it looked like an abandoned well. Its lip was made from piled up crumbling stones. I didn't approach it- I simply watched as he paused in front of it and looked to the Amazons just briefly before he stepped into it. He simply vanished. Without hesitation, Ortrera's warriors followed him. And our number was reduced by five.

Wordlessly, we headed for the border of Tartara. It was only a few minutes away. We could see it from here. On this side, Tartara was dark and horrible. A thin shroud of mist separated us from the other side, where we could see light and green fields. Ares turned around.

"Those who have not been condemned to Tartara can step right over the border without issue. It will prevent those who are damned."

"So…" I trailed off.

"So, it will prevent me from leaving," Hecate said, biting her lip as she looked around us. "But there appears to be a gate further down. Perhaps there is a guard?"

"You read my mind," Ares grinned. I shook my head. I had a feeling he was looking forward to a confrontation. It would be an outlet for his stress.

There was a guard and I was correct. Ares and Cadmus disappeared for a scant moment into the shadows and returned with their swords bloody. The difference between them was that Ares was smiling.

"The coast is clear," he announced.

We stepped through the gates to find the guards incapacitated. Only one was dead. The other appeared to be unconscious without a scratch on him. I looked at Cadmus.

"He'll awaken shortly," he explained. "I did not want to leave this gate unmanned. There is a reason that most are here."

"Good thinking," I replied, glancing around. No one approached yet, but I was certain it wouldn't be long. From what I had observed, the prisoners here were constantly looking for ways to escape.

Two steps later and we had left the bowels of the Underworld behind us. Five minutes more and the butterflies sent by Ahmose had found us once again, bringing their vitality with them. They hovered close to Aphrodite and I now, although since she and I passed the helm back and forth, it wasn't as imperative as it once was.

"We're surprisingly close to the oceans of Elyria," Hecate called behind her as she hurried ahead. "It won't take long."

She didn't exaggerate.

Less than an hour later, we faced beautiful fields of purple blossoms. Their scent was sweet and pungent and I inhaled, filling my lungs with the beautiful smell. The problem, however, was that the fields were empty.

This was most certainly where I had seen Empusa and Raquel in my visions, but there was nothing here now but for the flowers themselves.

"Empusa?" Hecate called hopefully. The only thing that moved were the blossoms with the gentle sea breeze. "Empusa?"

Nothing.

I stepped forward.

"Empusa?" I called. "You asked for my help and you told me to hurry. I'm here now. Can you come meet us?"

Nothing.

My shoulders slumped. I hadn't expected this. I had felt sure that when we arrived, they would be waiting. My heart constricted with an apprehension that I hadn't even known that I felt. I had thought I would see my daughter today. And I had been wrong.

"Mama?"

A little voice resounded through the air, carried by the wind. I turned in surprise to find Raquel running through the fields, her long dark hair streaming behind her. Empusa walked cautiously behind her, her face an unreadable mask.

"Raquel," I whispered weakly, before I took off running, plunging through the amethyst colored blooms to reach my daughter.

## Chapter Eleven

I clutched her little body close to mine, leaning down to inhale her. Her hair smelled like the outdoors, the ocean and little girl. She was thin enough that I could feel her shoulder blades beneath my fingers.

"I can't believe we found you," I cried as tears streaked down my face. "I was so afraid."

Her skinny little arms were clasped around my waist as she tilted her delicate face up to me, her bright green eyes shining.

"Empusa took care of me, Mama. She said you would be here as soon as you could. And she was right. Here you are."

Cadmus dropped to one knee next to her, pulling her into his strong arms. She was so small compared to him, so fragile and delicate. As he murmured to her, I turned to Empusa, who was just now approaching.

"Empusa," I called. "I can never repay you. Thank you so much for taking care of Raquel. Thank you."

She nodded and I couldn't help but notice how beautiful the girl was. She reminded me of a prima ballerina. She was so delicate. Her skin was clear and she possessed an otherworldly glow. Her hair was long and dark, curling delicately around her shoulders. But her eyes… they were the most unique eyes I had ever seen outside of my own. They were a multi-faceted gray with flecks of darker gray and green in them.

"You're welcome. I'm glad that you are receptive to visitors in your dreams and that you followed us here." She walked past me to her mother, into Hecate's waiting embrace.

"We've found you, too," Hecate said as she buried her face in her daughter's neck. Her shoulders quaked as she cried. "I can't believe that you've hidden from me for so long."

"I've been afraid," Empusa answered quietly. "I'm still afraid. So many things bubble just beneath the surface here. You've broken everything wide open. It is difficult to say what will happen."

"I can tell you what will happen," Hecate declared. "When this is finished with Zeus, you and I will go before Hades and he will uphold his bargain. He will retrieve your father and you will go free."

Empusa stared at her silently, her gray graze unfazed. "We shall see," she murmured.

"Yes, we shall," Hecate agreed determinedly. "And in the meantime, I brought you something." She reached into her cloak pocket and pulled out a bracelet. A pale moonstone shone mutely in the light. "Put this on. I have enchanted it to alert you when your father is near. Never take it off. It possesses other powers, also, but we can discuss that later."

"Thank you," Empusa murmured, stroking the stone lightly.

"Do you have shelter?" Ares asked. "We should get out of the open. Hades is undoubtedly in pursuit of us."

Empusa nodded. "Yes. There is a cave near the sea. No one has bothered us there for days and days."

"Then we should go there," Aphrodite piped up. She hadn't spoken in awhile- she had patiently walked along like the trooper that she could be. I had to admit, I was very proud of her.

Empusa nodded and led the way through the waving flowers. We followed in a joyful line. Finding Raquel was certainly a pick-me-up. I couldn't remember when I had been happier, even if I was still wandering through the Underworld.

At the end of the vast fields, the land sharply declined, leading to the sandy shores of the oceans of Elyria. I stood on the shores for a moment, staring at the water. I had always loved the water and standing next to an ocean always put things into perspective. It was so massive and wide that it made me feel insignificant. It reminded me that no matter what happened with me or in my life, the world would continue to turn, the oceans would continue to crash.

I pulled off my boots and stood with my toes buried in the sand, just where the lip of the water met the beach. The foam rolled over my feet and then retracted back into the ocean, a back and forth game of tug of war as the tide rolled in.

Cadmus joined me, with Raquel balanced on his shoulders. I had never seen a more beautiful sight. He looked perfectly at home with the child wrapped around him. If at all possible, it made me love him even more. While Raquel certainly looked more like me, there was a distinct resemblance to her father… something about the way her lips moved, maybe. I couldn't put my finger on it, but it was there. Right now, she leaned down and laughed into his ear and my heart warmed. They acted as though they had never been apart.

"Should we swim, mama?" Raquel asked me hopefully.

"No- don't!" Empusa interrupted from a few feet away. "There are Hydras swimming in these oceans—meant to guard Elyria and the isles from intruders."

I looked at Raquel. "Not now, sweet one. But we'll swim when we get home." She nodded happily, easily placated. "We need to find your cave, anyway. Can you show me?"

She nodded again and Cadmus set her down. She skipped joyfully away, looking back every once in awhile to make sure we were following. Cadmus grabbed my hand and we trailed behind her to the cave.

As caves went, it was fairly normal and nondescript. It yawned large and wide from the inlet of a cove. Empusa padded through the wet sand next to us, her filmy white skirt dragging in the surf.

"This is a safe place for us," she mentioned. "It is only accessible during the day. At night, the tide rolls in and blocks its entrance."

"Of course, that also means that you cannot leave it at night," Ortrera pointed out. Empusa shrugged delicately.

"I guess. If you want to look at it that way. To us, it meant protection."

"And I'm sure it will to us, also," I replied. "Thank you for bringing us here."

She looked at me for a second before she smiled and it lit up her entire face. She really was beautiful in a very delicate way. "You're welcome."

The inside was damp. Condensation formed on the ceiling and dripped into puddles on the ground. It smelled of wet sand, salt and rock, but it was cool enough that I shivered as we entered. Raquel bounced ahead.

"This is my bed, mama!" she cried, eager to show me. I quickly followed her to see and she led me to a small pallet at the back. "I don't like to sleep here, but Empusa told me that I had to at least rest."

"We all need to rest from time to time," I told her with a grin. "We'll put my blankets next to yours. Is that alright? Do you hog the bed?" She smiled shyly and shook her head.

"Well, that's good," Cadmus replied as he set our bags down. "Because your mother does and our bed is only so big. You must take after me." I slapped him playfully on the arm before realizing that I had just smacked his injured arm. I clapped my hand over my mouth.

"It's alright, wife," he assured me. "I feel much better. The helm has allowed me to heal. I'm sure that Hecate could remove the stitches if she has a free minute."

"I'll do it in a bit," she called from the front of the cave.

"Take your time," Cadmus called back. "I'm in no rush. I'm not going anywhere."

"You might want to come up here," Hecate suggested. "Empusa is sharing interesting things."

Cadmus and I looked at each other. I knelt next to Raquel. "Can you look through my knapsack and get some soft, dry wraps and arrange a sleeping pallet for me next to yours?"

She nodded. "Because you don't want me to hear what Empusa says?"

I laughed. "You're a smart little thing. I don't want you to be afraid. We're here now and you don't have to worry about anything."

She launched herself into my arms, hugging me tightly before she stepped back.

"I love you, mama."

My heart melted as I stared at my beautiful child.

"I love you, too," I whispered, too afraid to trust my voice to speak louder. It was the first time she had said that to me.

Cadmus wiped a tear from my cheek that I hadn't even known that I had shed before he leaned over and kissed it. And then we hurried to the front of the cave to join the group that had congregated around Hecate's daughter.

"The gods are definitely still here?" Hecate asked, her gaze frozen on her daughter.

Empusa nodded. "Yes, I've heard talks of them. They are on the Isles of the Blessed."

I looked at Hecate. "You act as though you knew that they were here at one time." I raised an eyebrow. She looked at me sheepishly.

"I did know that. But I never would have dreamed that Hades would have kept them there. This is very strange. I would have thought he would have hidden them more securely."

"Perhaps now would be a good time for you to explain exactly what happened…what you did to assist Hades," Aphrodite suggested gently. "We will not hold it against you, but I think we need to know."

Hecate looked pained as she stared past us, but she nodded.

"Alright. You already know that they promised me that if I helped them, they would release the curse on Empusa- that they would put it back where it belonged on Mormo. So, I agreed to help with whatever asked me to do. I would have done anything."

"And what did you end up doing?" I prompted.

"As you know, if you eat in the Underworld, you are constrained here. Hades created a duplicate Mount Olympus on the Isles of the Blessed- Zeus' palace was replicated to the smallest detail. With my magic, I bewitched the doorways of Zeus' banquet hall to become a temporary portal to the Underworld and they were transported to the Isles of Blessed, unknowingly of course. They thought they were on Olympus. They ate, drank and were merry… and they didn't even realize what had happened until late in the night. It was a brilliant plan, I have to admit. Hades thought of every detail."

"But you carried it out," I asked sadly. She nodded.

"Yes. His plan was successful because of me."

"But since they have eaten here, they will be imprisoned here," Aphrodite said, her lovely voice shaking. "How can we un-do that?"

"I do not know," Hecate said miserably. "There must be a way, however."

"Well, we shall all think on it," Ares instructed. "But for now, we must rest for a while. We are all weary and we know what we must do next."

"We do?" I asked warily. The expression on Ares' face was too joyful to bode well for the rest of us.

"Of course we do," he replied. "We must cross the oceans of Elyria."

"Of course we must," I sighed. "You do realize that it contains Hydras?"

"Yep," he answered happily. I sighed again.

But I was distracted by shadows in the mouth of the cave. I looked up to find Annen, Ahmose, Alexi, Eris and the four Amazon warriors who had accompanied Annen to the Spiritlands.

"That was quick," Ares commended them. "Welcome."

I took one look at Ahmose's grim face and knew something was wrong.

"What is it?" I asked quickly. He wearily studied me for a moment, probably assessing my state of mind.

"I'm fine," I snapped. "What is wrong?"

"It's your mother," he answered simply. "Your mortal mother. She has been taken from Calypso's island."

I gasped and I felt my knees go weak.

"I should have known," I muttered. "I should have known that he would do something like this."

"There's no way you could have," Cadmus soothed me. "Ogygia was the safest place for her."

"Apparently it wasn't," I replied.

"This does not change anything," Ares said. "Our course of action must remain the same. We will travel to the isles to see Zeus. Hades will show himself at some point and reveal what he wants."

"He wants me," I answered limply. "He wants to keep me here."

"Well, he can't have you," Cadmus growled. "He'll have to learn that the hard way."

I smiled what I knew was a weak smile. They hadn't seen how determined Hades was.

"I can't wait," I told everyone. "I would never be able to sleep anyway, knowing that he has my mother. I'm sure she's terrified. Can we leave now, please?"

"There is a boat," Empusa offered. "It's very old, but it is large. It's moored down the coast a ways away. I do not know whose it is."

"I think it is meant for those who are granted access to Elysia," Aphrodite said. "That is how I remember it anyway. I think that all who earn the privilege of spending eternity in paradise must pass that one final test. Anyone who is good and true and possesses the purest of hearts can pass the oceans safely. The Hydras will not harm them. When it dispatches its passengers in the isles, the boat will sail itself back to the coast, to await the next passenger."

"That is correct," Hecate confirmed. "That is the way it has always been."

"Well, then," Ares proclaimed. "Let us go. I am an amazing sailor."

I rolled my eyes at Raquel, who had edged up to my side. "Your grandfather thinks that he is amazing at everything," I told her. She eyed him. His bulging muscles glistened in the light from the mouth of the cave. He was large, strong, handsome and assured. She looked back to me.

"Is he not?" she asked innocently.

I sighed. "I suppose he is. But it would be nice if he wasn't quite so aware of it." She giggled, then grasped my hand.

"Is everything going to be alright?" she asked nervously. I dropped to one knee and stared into her eyes.

"Everything will be fine," I assured her. "I promise."

My words echoed throughout the cave, reiterating my assurance.

"Let us go!" Ares called impatiently. I held Raquel's hand and dutifully followed everyone to the beach.

When Empusa said 'boat', she probably should have said 'ship'. It was enormous. Large and wooden, it creaked in the shallow water by the shore, its hull covered in barnacles and moss. White sails were rolled in the masts and lines whipped in the wind. Strangely, it didn't appear to be anchored, it simply stayed where it was.

"Are you sure you can sail that?" I asked Ares uncertainly. He glowered at me.

"You doubt your father?" he asked indignantly. "Of course I can sail it." He stomped ahead and as he plunged through the shallow water, a rope ladder dropped over the side of the ship.

I raised an eyebrow and turned to my husband.

"Fun, right?" he grinned.

"Yeah, fun," I sighed. "Not exactly what I was thinking… but what can you do?"

"Carry on, I suppose," he replied, unbothered. "On that note…" he reached for Raquel and he helped her climb onto the ladder.

While everyone was preoccupied, Empusa crept up behind me. "It's starting," she whispered. "I cannot stay here. I am too afraid of my father. No matter what happens, he will not stop hunting me until he kills me. Please tell my mother that I love her."

Before I had a chance to even respond, she was running down the coast, splashing through the water. I inhaled sharply. Hecate wasn't going to take this well. I sighed and grabbed the bottom rung of the ladder and pulled myself up the side.

Hecate looked behind me, then back to me, puzzled. "Where is Empusa?"

"She ran away," I answered softly. "She was afraid and said to tell you that she loved you. Hecate, once this is done, we can find her. We'll set things right."

Hecate's face drained of color, but she simply nodded, sinking into a nearby bench seat. She pulled her knees up to her chin and sat silently watching the water. I turned from her, unable to stand the pain on her face, and looked around.

It was sparse on board. Bench seating lined the sides and the hull was open. Ares unfurled the sails and shortly thereafter, we were gaining speed as we sailed into the vast oceans. Before we knew it, there was nothing around for miles except for the sparkling water. Ares learned shortly after we set sail that he didn't need to do anything at all... the ship sailed itself. He and my mother sat curled up on a bench, talking quietly amongst themselves.

Cadmus was engaged in a conversation with Ahmose, so I settled onto the very tip of the bow with Raquel situated on my lap. The wind whipped our hair away from our faces as our boat plunged ahead, riding the waves with abandon. My daughter's slight body sagged against me and I smiled into her hair.

"You can sleep, little one," I told her. "It will take awhile to get there."

"I'm not sleepy, mama," she insisted. I smiled again.

Cadmus and Ahmose moved closer to me.

"Wife, Ahmose shared some interesting information with me," Cadmus said quietly.

"I don't know how much more 'interesting' information I want to hear," I replied wryly.

"This is truly interesting," he answered, his face slightly bothered. My curiosity was piqued in spite of myself.

"What is it?"

"Well, as you know, Annen and I are brothers," Ahmose began, his ancient voice tired and hoarse. "We have been the advisors to Zeus for a very long time."

"I did learn that, yes," I answered. "And?"

"And when Zeus rendered you mortal, he sent Annen and I with you, to protect you and to protect the bloodstone."

"Yes, we knew that also," I replied. "What is the interesting part?"

"If you stop interrupting, I'll get to it," Ahmose reprimanded lightly. I smiled. This was the Ahmose that I knew. Crotchety and no-nonsense.

"The Fates and the Keres each had their own agendas, and they each sought to use Annen and I to further their causes. Between the two sets of sisters, we were threatened many times and ultimately, it came down to us having to outwit them all by playing their own game. We were under orders by Zeus to guide and protect you.

"You, however, were so completely manipulated by the Fates, that we had to divide in order to conquer. We were not meant to share the truth with you. So, for every time the Fates used you to make horrible decisions for their entertainment, Annen used Cadmus to try and un-do those decisions."

I was still for a moment, trying to process that. I turned to Cadmus.

"Annen came to you, as Ahmose came to me?"

He nodded. "But I only vaguely remember it."

"You pitted us against each other?" I was aghast.

"But not for our entertainment," he hastened to add. "Only because you were being manipulated. Your decisions were not the wise choices that you thought them to be. We did our best, but usually, you were so determined to carry through with your missions, you did everything you could to make sure that the Fates' wishes were kept. You are a very loyal person, Harmonia."

"Cadmus and I were working against each other and didn't even know it?" I was floored.

"Neither of you knew it," Ahmose confirmed. "Zeus knew that when the time was right, you would come to realize who you were… and when that happened, the prophecy would be upheld."

"My love, you've always been so good and true," I murmured, twisting around to cup my husband's face with one hand. "I'm sorry that I was stubborn."

"You stubbornly upheld your ideals," he corrected me. "You thought you were doing the right thing. If the Fates are never released from Tartara, that will be fine with me."

"Mama, look!" Raquel interrupted, pointing into the water. I peered over the side and instantly recoiled.

Enormous black sea monsters were swimming in circles around our boat. The hair stood up on my neck and goosebumps formed everywhere on my body.

"Hydras," I whispered.

"There is no need to fear," Hecate soothed us. "While it is true that we were not granted permission to enter Elyria, our hearts are true. The Hydras will not bother us if that is the case."

"How do we know that everyone is true?" Ares demanded, his face dark. "Betrayal is an epidemic, I am afraid."

"Let's not do this again," I replied in frustration. "Ares, every one of us here has made decisions that we regret, including you."

"Does anyone have anything to hide?" Hecate asked the group. "Share it now, if you do."

Everyone remained silent. I looked into the water again, just in time to see the tip of one long scaly tail disappear under the boat. Within a few seconds, the nose of the same beast reappeared. They were still swimming circles, but they were not bothering us.

"I think Hecate is right," I breathed. "I think we are fine. They have not bothered us yet."

My daughter was unfazed by the giant creatures and in fact, she seemed almost mesmerized by them as she watched them swim fluidly beneath us. Cadmus and I exchanged amused looks above her head. Simply observing her was a joy to us. She was such an unexpected blessing to both of us.

Weariness began to take its toll on me, however, and I leaned against my husband, absorbing his strength. He leaned forward, pressing a warm kiss to my forehead.

"Sleep, my love," he suggested. I nodded, closing my eyes.

The next thing I knew, Raquel was shouting.

My eyes blinked open and we were approaching land. I rubbed at my eyes and turned to Cadmus.

"How long was I asleep?"

"A few hours," he replied. "You needed it."

"Did you rest?" I asked.

"I'm a warrior," he answered, as though that were answer enough. I rolled my eyes.

"And warriors don't need rest, apparently," I muttered. From my periphery, I saw him smile. I didn't dwell on his arrogance though. I had to admit, it was one of the things I loved about him. Instead, I turned my attention to the beauty that faced us.

The coast was lined with tropical plants and palm trees. I could practically smell the coconuts in the sea breeze that lightly ruffled my hair. The sand was white, the water was blue and calm. There was no sign of the Hydras now as we glided smoothly through the water to come to a rest in the soft sand by the shore.

I had never smelled anything like the air here. Clean and crisp, it tasted of salt and rich flower blossoms. Brightly colored tropical birds rested in the trees above us. The temperature was just right- not too warm and not too cool.

"Welcome to paradise," Hecate said. As she did, the ladder uncoiled from the floor of the boat and dropped to the water below. She wasted no time in climbing over the side. One by one, we all waited our turn to climb off the ship and within minutes, we stood on the perfect sands of the beach.

"Mon dieu," Aphrodite murmured, gazing up and down the lengths of the coast. "What beauty!"

"It doesn't compare to you, my love," Ares announced, bowing low as he swept up her hand and kissed it. Aphrodite smiled and kissed him soundly before returning her attention to the shore.

"I've never actually been here before. I should have come long ago."

"It is said that this is a place of perfection," Hecate said quietly. "And I personally believe that to be true. The weather is always perfect, there is no strife or hate. It is most certainly a perfection."

I couldn't argue. It was the most beautiful place I had ever seen. But somehow, it seemed vaguely familiar.

"I feel as though I've been here before," I murmured to no one in particular. Ahmose stared at me in consternation.

"I will be so happy when your memories are fully returned to you," he replied. "Of course you have been here. Once upon a time, Zeus sent you and Cadmus to live here. You appealed to his generous nature and asked that due to all of your misfortune with your necklace if you could be sent from Olympus. He agreed and sent you to live here, until the time when he needed to retrieve you so that he could render you mortal."

"We were removed from this paradise to live tragic lives in the mortal world again and again?" I was incredulous. Our story just seemed to get worse and worse as more was added to it. Ahmose nodded wordlessly. There was nothing more to be said. It was bad enough as it was.

"I don't remember it at all," Cadmus said quietly to me. "But I wish that I did."

"I'm not sure," I mused. "I'm beginning to wish that I didn't have any of my old memories. They cause nothing but pain."

I was thinking of his betrayal and he knew it. He stared at me regretfully and pulled me to his chest.

"I'm so sorry, Harmonia. If I could change everything, I would. I promise you- I would."

"I know," I murmured. To our right, Raquel explored the coastline terrain, marveling at the beautiful birds and plump fruit.

"Don't eat it!" several of us cried at once. She turned to us with an impish grin.

"I won't," she called back. "But I'd like to."

"As would I," Ares grumbled. "I'm hungry enough to eat an entire Pegasus." He glanced at Ortrera. "Don't scowl at me, daughter. I wouldn't eat *yours*."

Appeased, Ortrera and her warriors splashed through the shallow water to make their way to land. Cadmus, Ahmose, Annen and I followed behind, followed by Alexi and Eris, both of whom had remained strangely quiet.

Something occurred to me and I turned to Eris.

"A person has to be true of heart to approach these islands," I observed. "And you passed the test. How did you do that?"

"I do not know," she answered honestly. "I have no malice in me at the moment. All I am focused on is getting Alexi's soul back."

"So you are focused on doing good for someone else," I mused. "Perhaps that is what did it." She shrugged her shoulders. I knew that her change of heart was only temporary. After Alexi was restored, I was certain that she would be back to her old, conniving ways soon enough. As my polar opposite, her very nature was one that relished discord and discontentment. There was no changing that.

"We should go," Hecate called to us from the tree line. "We have things to do."

That we did. We all fell into line and followed her into the trees and through the tropics. Each step led us somewhere even more beautiful. It was difficult to comprehend. Green vines wrapped around luscious trees and flowers. Birds sang quietly, but not too loudly.

I had to agree with Ares. I was starving. It was difficult to resist plucking a piece of ripe fruit from a vine and eating it. But we did. We simply kept walking.

And soon enough, the jungle-like foliage gave way to fields of waving plants and flowers. With every movement, their lush scents were tossed into the air. There were beautiful homes scattered here and there among the sloping hills and a tranquil river flowed in the middle.

Hecate marched right for the river. Trustingly, we walked a trail along the side until we came to a pristine pier. A string of boats were moored there and she stepped into one, careful not to rock it overly much. Annen and Ahmose joined her. The rest of us separated into several other boats. Hecate turned the nose of her little watercraft to head into the river and paddled fluidly along.

"Where are we going?" I called.

She paused her rowing and turned to look over her shoulder. "To the most beautiful island you've ever seen."

I paused in surprise. "Aren't we already there?"

She laughed. "No, Chosen One. These are the Elysian Fields. They lead up to the Isles. The isles are even better than this!"

I could scarcely imagine it. As we rowed, I watched the sides of the river. Every once in awhile, a person would stop and stare back at us. I was fairly certain that I recognized Hercules. He was fishing on the banks, his enormous muscles bulging larger than any I had ever seen, including my husband's or father's.

"Isn't that…" I breathed.

"Yes," Cadmus confirmed, without missing a stroke of his oar. "That is Hercules. Reattach your eyes, Harmonia. It's just muscle."

"A *lot* of muscle," I corrected. "Wow."

Cadmus shook his head good-naturedly, but he didn't mind. He was confident in his worth. He was everything to me and he was twice as beautiful as Hercules.

The river carried us gently for miles before it opened up into a wide lake. From here, I could see that across the lake, there were islands.

"The Isles of the Blessed," I said needlessly.

Everyone around me was staring in fascination. In the middle of the islands, a majestic mountain rose from the ground, sweeping so high that it seemed to touch the white clouds.

"Olympus," I murmured. Or rather, the duplicate Olympus. It was where the gods were being held. A sense of urgency came over me and I wanted nothing more than to hurry and get there. Everything that we had been through up until this point could be resolved if we could just free Zeus. The moment we had been waiting for was upon us.

# Chapter Twelve

This was beyond anything I could have imagined.

As we traveled through the look-alike Olympus, the similarities... no, the duplicity was incredible. Hades had thought of every last detail and had supplied it. No wonder the Olympians had thought they were in Zeus' banquet hall and had allowed themselves to be deceived. Everything here was identical to the ancient city in the Spiritlands. If I didn't know better, I would swear that I was there right now.

But I was not. I was here.

And here was... fascinating. I couldn't help but hang my mouth open in amazement as we passed quaint shops, mouth-watering restaurants, dress makers, tailors... all identical to things that existed on Olympus. There were even blue lotus blossoms drifting down from trees in the air, falling gently across the cobblestone streets. I cast out a hand and allowed one to drift onto my palm.

"Don't eat it," Cadmus warned.

"I won't," I murmured. "It's just so... everything is..."

"Unbelievable," Aphrodite breathed, staring around us in awe.

"My thoughts exactly," I agreed. A random thought occurred to me and I turned to Hecate, dropping the flower onto the cobblestone street.

"Hecate, you said that you created a portal from Zeus' own banquet hall to here. Does it still exist?"

She nodded. "It does. But it is closed and they wouldn't be able to use it anyway. They have eaten here so they must remain."

"I know," I replied softly. "I was just wondering about it."

"If I open it, *we* can use it," she answered knowingly, understanding my question. "But not them."

"Not them," I repeated quietly, pondering that. "It must have been so strange for them all of this time… being trapped here in this identical world, never being able to get home… especially with the portal right beneath their fingers. They simply couldn't use it."

"They are not accustomed to being rendered helpless, either," Cadmus interjected. "I still can't quite believe that you managed to carry this off. I can't believe that Zeus allowed himself to be deceived. It's almost unfathomable."

"He knew it would happen," Hecate reminded him. "He had seen it coming long before it happened. He just didn't know how or when. He was constantly watching for it. We simply used an approach that he didn't expect."

"And who would expect this?" I asked, still staring around me in wonder. "This is incredible."

Hecate didn't seem impressed. But then again, she probably just harbored regret over the part she played in putting the gods here. I couldn't blame her. I would feel the same way. So rather than rubbing salt in her wound and continuing to gush about the wonders around us, I fell silent.

We made our way quickly through the city and up the winding road to the palace. Pristine and sprawling, it was exactly like its authentic counterpart. Massive marble columns lined the porches and walkways, manicured lawns stretched as far as the eye could see and thousands of windows sparkled in the light.

As I stood still and looked upward at this beautiful building, I suddenly felt apprehensive. Would Hades be waiting for us inside? He had to know that we would find our way here. Was this a set-up or a trap? I took a deep breath, but I didn't see what choice we had. We had to continue.

In typical fashion, Ares barged onward, up the wide steps and to the front doors. He didn't knock, he simply entered. To my shock, the doors weren't locked. That seemed strange and only increased my unease.

As we filed into the palace, it was easy to pretend that we were entering the real palace on the real Olympus. The rooms were sparkling clean, the stone floors buffed and polished. Windows stretched floor to ceiling, elegant and lavish furniture was artfully arranged in every room with beautiful art adorning the walls.

But each room was empty.

"Where is everyone?" Aphrodite murmured as we made our way quietly through the rooms.

"The dungeon?" Ortrera suggested.

"Most likely," I agreed. "We should head that way."

As we turned into the next hall, we finally encountered another person, a young servant girl with her arms full of fresh towels.

"You, there!" Ares called, motioning to her. "Where is everyone?"

She seemed startled to find strangers walking toward her, but she didn't run away. She approached us with a timid expression.

"They're in the courtyard, sir," she replied meekly, her head bowed.

"The courtyard?" Ares' brow was furrowed. "Very well. Thank you."

She nodded and scurried on her way as we looked at each other anxiously. The courtyard? Perhaps this was a trap after all. Maybe an ambush was waiting for us outside. We would have to tread carefully.

Ares and Cadmus led the way through the remaining part of the castle and within a few minutes, we spilled out the back doors onto the terrace that led to the courtyards.

"What the hell...." Ares stopped talking as confusion overtook him.

The gods were having a party.

Long lantern strings were hung festively from tree to tree, swinging gently in the breeze. Elaborate flower arrangements and fruit adorned each long banquet table, while large lotus blossoms drifted down upon the banquet attendees. In the middle, several gods were dancing and everyone here was laughing and having a wonderful time while Zeus and Hera looked on from the head table.

"What is the meaning of this?" Ares roared.

Everyone stopped moving and turned our way. I suddenly felt self-conscious, as though we had just crashed a party instead of staging an elaborate rescue maneuver. I felt my cheeks flush as every silver eye in the courtyard fixed upon us. Zeus' ancient face lit up as he saw us, his eyes crinkling at the corners as he smiled.

"Ares," Zeus called happily. "Come forward, my friend. It's been a long time. Aphrodite, it is nice to see your lovely face." His silver eyes scanned the rest of the group and halted when they found me. "And Harmonia. I am so pleased that you have been victorious."

"Victorious?" I asked hesitantly. "I was given no choice."

He nodded. "I know, sweet girl. My apologies. But it was the only way. I hope you see that. And now that you're here, you can feast with us. Come. Join us! It's beautiful here. We have not a care in the world."

He waved his hand and the dancers began dancing again. I studied the scene in front of me warily. Zeus' demeanor was strange. He was as light and carefree as I had ever seen him. His face, which was usually serious and lined with worry-lines, was relaxed and he was actually smiling. I looked at him uncertainly and felt everyone with me do the same.

"Mother?" I whispered. "What is going on?"

"I don't know," she replied, not taking her gaze from the festivities.

"Nothing, sweet girl," Zeus called from across the courtyard. He had heard me and I startled. How was that possible? Our gifts were blocked here in the Underworld.

"Not for us," Zeus replied again with a wide grin. "We have an unlimited supply of nectar here that perpetuates our gifts. Life is good."

He could also read our minds. We all realized it at the same time. Without our gifts, we weren't able to block our thoughts and I suddenly had the uneasy thought that we might actually need to.

"No, you do not," Zeus replied indignantly. "Why would that be the case?"

"I don't know," I answered calmly. "This is just all very strange to me. We have traveled through hell and high water to get to you- *to save you-* and now that we have arrived, we see that you're having a party, as happy as larks. I find that curious, to say the least."

Zeus' stare flitted from me to Hecate and for a split second, it hardened, and then he relaxed once again.

"Hecate," he drawled slowly. Her shoulders slumped as he spoke, weighed down by her every contributing action that had put them here. "I should be angry with you, but I am not. I'll admit I was furious in the beginning, but we have found joy here. You cannot imagine how wonderful it is to bear no responsibility for the world at all. We are free to simply enjoy our own lives. So, perhaps I should thank you instead."

"You speak as if you like it here," Ares replied uncertainly, shock evidenced on his face. I was certain it was mirrored on my own.

Zeus shrugged. "Tis the truth, we do."

"But you can't leave," I pointed out, still in shock.

"No, we can't. But why would we want to? We have everything we need. You should see for yourselves. Stay with us!"

"You can't be serious!" I snapped. "After everything you have put us through- for thousands of years- in order to secure your rescue, you can sit there and nonchalantly dismiss it and tell us that life is wonderful here? If life is so wonderful here, you should have simply volunteered to come in the first place and saved the rest of us a bunch of heartache."

"Harmonia," Aphrodite began warningly.

"What, mother?" I replied angrily. "What is he going to do? He apparently doesn't care that he has abdicated his reign. I can't show him respect right now because I don't feel it."

"She's right, Aphrodite," Ares declared. "This is rubbish. All of it." He stomped through the festival-goers and stood in front of Zeus, leaning down to speak directly into his face. "You have wronged us, Zeus."

Zeus appraised him quietly and then nodded. "You are correct. I have. It was not meant that way, you understand. We were tricked into entrapment here, but as the years passed, we settled into life here. There are no power struggles, no corruption, no hate. Hades leaves us be, he simply enjoys the powerful energy that we garner with our presence. There is nothing to dislike, and I cannot imagine ever wanting to return to the Spiritlands."

His statement caused most of us to drop our mouths open. This couldn't be happening. Everything that we had been through… had been for this? It was unfathomable. And to make it worse, Zeus didn't seem to care.

"Come now," he called to the rest of us. "Come and catch us up on the latest goings-on. We'll be interested to learn how you have managed to topple the Fates."

His words brought an interesting point back to mind.

"Zeus," I began, "With the Fates' overthrown and you here in the Underworld, there is no one at the helm, so to speak. There is no one to monitor the mortal world, no one to regulate the Spiritlands. This is just… irresponsible. You must return. You are the only one who can use your sword correctly. We tried and failed miserably, making some things even worse in the process. We need you to set everything to rights."

He stared at me like I had two heads.

"There is something that I have learned since I have been here, Harmonia, something monumental. It doesn't matter if we interfere or not, life… whether it be mortals or gods… goes on without us. We might bend something to our will, but that does not mean that the way it would have gone on its own would have been any less right. We are unnecessary," he concluded simply. "I believe that we have out-lived our purpose."

"You have given up," I replied, drawing my own conclusions. "You have simply given up."

"No," he shook his head. "That is not the case. What I have just told you is the truth. And if you had been cognizant of your surroundings and your true self all of these years, you would have come to this same realization. Fate… destiny… those are simply words that we use to fool ourselves with. Neither of those things exists. Every person takes their own lives into their own hands, they make their own decisions. We are not needed for that. We only thought that we were."

"So, it's all just been a big misunderstanding?" I snapped sarcastically. "For all of these years, we've been deluded and living a lie? I can't believe what I'm hearing."

Cadmus laid his hand soothingly on my arm, a silent warning to check myself- to remain calm. I glanced down and swallowed. Then swallowed again. He was right. It would do no good to lose my temper with this god of gods. I took a deep breath.

"Harmonia," Zeus said calmly. "You cannot leave right now at any rate. There is much to be discussed and you will need to determine a way to leave. Stay. Drink nectar- you all need it, I am sure."

His grandfatherly face was placid and unbothered, his silver hair thick and unruly as usual. He remained seated with his wife, waiting for our reply. I nodded curtly. It would certainly be nice to take in nectar. We could use our gifts back.

"Wonderful!" Zeus said warmly. "We shall show you to your rooms."

"I think we can find them ourselves," I answered. "We know the way."

"That you do," he nodded. "That you do."

We retreated from the courtyard silently, making our way back into the large, empty palace and stood in a tired group, looking at each other dazedly.

"Did that even just happen?" I asked. "It doesn't seem possible. If they do not want to return, if they do not want to retake their rightful places, then what will happen?"

Hecate shook her head slowly. "This is not something that I ever foresaw. I have no notion of what to do. In all of my travels here in the Underworld, Hades never allowed me access here, and I didn't want it. I thought the gods would be furious with me and I didn't want to face that. This… this is not what I expected. I'm sorry that I wasn't able to provide you with warning."

"Do you think they've been bewitched?" Aphrodite asked. "That would at least make sense."

Ares nodded slowly in agreement. "That would indeed make sense. Hecate, what do you think? Is that a possibility?"

She appeared to consider that. "I do not know. I don't know how it would have been done."

I remembered how each silver gaze had fixated on me- not intensely as would have been the case once upon a time, but instead, very relaxed and complacent. They were simply curious at our arrival.

I shook my head. "I don't think so. I think they've just grown lazy here. They've grown used to this way of life and they think there is no reason for them to return. From their point of view, they've been here for thousands of years with no negative effects on the world. They just don't realize…"

Cadmus rubbed my back. "We'll talk with them again tomorrow, Harmonia. For now, let us get a drink and some rest. We all desperately need it. Ortrera's warriors look dead on their feet. They've been guarding us constantly without sleep."

"We're fine," Ortrera insisted, although her face was tired and worn.

"Of course you are," I answered with a small grin. "Sister, it is not a weakness to grow weary. You haven't slept in days."

She dismissed my concern with a scowl and a shake of her head, so I let it drop. The Amazons were proud to a fault. They would rather die than admit what they considered a weakness.

I trailed my hand on the polished banister as we climbed the majestic staircase. I couldn't remember the last time I had been so tired myself. Raquel clung to my other hand, still looking around in bewilderment. If it was hard for me to comprehend, it must be near impossible for her.

There was no way we were going to let her out of our sight, so we kept her in the same bedroom with us, snuggling her into the middle of the bed. As we climbed in next to her, Cadmus on one side and me on the other, I stroked her dark hair away from her face.

"Everything will be fine now," I whispered to her. "We're safe. We'll sleep and then figure out what we're going to do next."

"But what about Hades, Mama?" she asked, her eyes widening in anxiety. "Empusa said that he could be anywhere at any given time and I know that he is looking for us. Why does he want us?"

I thought for a minute about what to say. Hades was a very complex person, as were his intentions. Finally, I replied.

"Hades is complicated," I began. "I don't believe that he is all bad. He has his own priorities and sometimes, I think he has lost touch with human values."

"But he's not human, he's a god," Raquel pointed out.

"I know. But even as gods, we have human emotions. Hades allows his to become blurred sometimes. He gets blinded by trying to get what he wants... which is bringing more people to join him here in the Underworld. The more people who are here, the more energy this place has. I think that's where the light comes from in Erebus. If you notice, there is no light at all in Tartara- because the souls there are black. The souls in Erebus are neither good nor bad, so there is a muted, soft light from their energy. But here in the Isles, the light is as bright as sunshine. And I think that can only be because the souls here are the purest and the best. Hades values this. He wants our energy."

"Even mine?" Raquel's voice was tiny.

"Probably. But don't you worry," Cadmus said fiercely. "He can't have you. I will protect you with my life. And your father is a warrior."

"One of the best," I agreed proudly. "Has he ever told you of the dragons that he has slayed?"

She shook her head, her eyes wide. I snuggled closer and listened to Cadmus' husky voice tell tales of his own bravery as I drifted off to sleep.

I immediately wished that I was still awake.

In my dream, I was in a dark, scary place filled with shadows and the sound of dripping water. I knew right away that I had been summoned here, although I couldn't imagine by whom. Everyone who usually came to me in dreams was here with me now, including Ahmose. I didn't have to wait long to find out.

"Oh, Harmonia," a deep, velvety voice said from behind me. I spun around to find Hades stepping from the shadows. He was as handsome as ever with his dark eyes glinting as he appraised me. "Did you think that I wouldn't find you?"

He didn't sound angry. He sounded very patient. I took a step back. I had learned one thing. Nothing was ever what it seemed. If he seemed calm and patient, it was most likely that he was the exact opposite.

He threw his head back and laughed.

"I do so enjoy you, Harmonia. I'm not going to rage against you. Why would I do that? There are much more genteel ways to get what I want."

"Such as?" I asked nervously.

"We'll get to that," he promised. "For now, let me look at you." He walked closer and stepped directly in front of me, reaching out to grasp my chin. Turning it this way and that, he examined me.

"Flushed cheeks, sparkling eyes, refreshed skin," he observed. "Someone has been drinking nectar again."

"Only a sip before bed," I replied warily.

"Oh, I am not condemning you," he assured me. "Of course not. It is exactly what I would expect. And you look refreshed and lovely. Did you enjoy your visit with the Olympians?"

He studied me innocently, waiting for me to explode. I didn't give him the satisfaction.

"Why, yes. We did. It wasn't what we expected, but we can work with it. So few things in life are as expected."

He moved closer and inhaled my neck and I found that his nearness made me woozy. What was it about him that drew me in like this? Whenever I was not with him, I didn't struggle with thinking about him. It was only a condition that popped up in his presence. The term 'animal magnetism' didn't begin to cover it.

"I'm glad you feel that way," he said with a sly grin, reading my thoughts. "I'm extremely attracted to you, as well. You've occupied my thoughts ever since you arrived. Your beauty, your innocence, your purity. Think of what you and I could accomplish together, little one. Think on that."

"Persephone wouldn't enjoy that," I pointed out. "She gave me the helm so that I could escape to prevent that very thing."

His lip twisted into a snarl for just a moment before he composed himself again.

"Yes, the helm. We shall get to that, as well."

"Hades, you're very handsome. It is true. And whenever I am near you, you do something that makes me feel almost unbearably attracted to you. But I know that you are somehow inflicting that reaction in me. I love my husband more than life itself. I would never choose you over him. So, whatever you are plotting, put it out of your head. I won't agree to it."

"No?" he asked in amusement. "I do so love your passion, Harmonia. It is one of the things that draws me to you. But you must learn to not be so impetuous. You cannot react to any situation with certainty until you know all of the extenuating circumstances."

"Such as?" I raised an eyebrow.

He held out his elbow and I stared at him unmoving.

"You really think I will just walk with you?"

"Would you like to see your mortal mother?" he asked simply. My jaw dropped. In my utter weariness and all of the excitement and stress of finding the Olympians, I had momentarily forgotten what Ahmose had told me- that my mother had disappeared from Ogygia.

"What have you done?" I demanded. In answer, he held out his elbow again. Gritting my teeth, I took it and we strolled slowly further into the dark abyss that surrounded us. We didn't need to go far

Three glittering golden cages stood in the middle of the room. They were beautiful, with ivy garlands wrapped around the bars festively. Inside each one, a shadowy figure sat. I crept closer to see more clearly and gasped.

Not only did he have my mother, but my best friends from the mortal world, Jess and Jenn Gray were here as well. I yanked free of him and ran to the cages.

"Mom!" I cried as I pulled at her bars. But even with my goddess strength, they didn't budge. Allison Lockhart eyed me calmly.

"Hi sweetie! Have you come to join us?"

I froze. She didn't seem bothered or afraid. I looked into her cage, and saw that it extended magically into a set of lavish bedchambers. It only appeared as gilded cage. I shook my head.

"Mom, are you alright?"

She looked at me strangely. "Of course I am, sweetie. I've never been better."

Confusion clouded my thoughts as I turned to my friends.

"Jess? Jenn?" I asked warily. "Are you alright?"

Jess gave me her signature sassy look, her little pixie nose tilted into the air. "Why in the world wouldn't we be, Macy? I'm ticked though because you have never shared this place with me. Hades says that you have known him a long time. And I'm supposed to be your best friend. You've been holding out on me."

"Holding out on you?" I repeated uncertainly as dread filled me up. What in the hell was going on here?

Hades crooked one finger at Jess and she eagerly jumped from her seat, throwing open her cage door and flinging herself into his waiting arms. He kissed her long and lustfully as she curled her body around his. He glanced up at me as Jess sighed contentedly.

"What have you done to them?" I whispered. "Hades? This is… this is atrocious."

He withdrew from Jess and motioned for her to return to her cage. She sighed, but obediently returned, glaring at me as she passed.

"Why is it atrocious, Macy?" she snapped. "Are you jealous?"

"Jealous?" I repeated. I turned to Jenn. "Jenn… surely you don't feel the same way."

"What way do you mean, Macy?" she turned to me innocently. "We love it here. Why wouldn't we?" She sounded puzzled. "No homework, Hades is amazing…and we feel perfect, all of the time."

"But you're prisoners," I pointed out. They all three shook their heads in unison.

"We can go anywhere here that we wish," my mom answered proudly. "Not at first, but we proved ourselves. We showed Hades that we don't want to leave, so now we're free to roam as we wish."

My gaze flew to Hades. "I don't know what is going on here, but you need to release them. They don't belong here." I tuned out their protests as I focused on the god of the Underworld. "I don't know what you've done to them, but stop."

He looked at me in dark amusement. "Sweet Harmonia. It is not something that I've 'done', it is just the way that I am. I cannot help it. The attraction that you feel toward me? Amplify that by at least a thousand. That is how mortals feel when I am near." He shrugged. "It is just the way it is. They are attracted to me, almost uncontrollably. They can't help it and neither can I. It is just something about me."

"It is one of your abilities," I whispered in realization. "It is how you draw people here and keep them."

He smiled at me silently, his teeth blindingly white. I found that I had to fight the strange attraction to him myself… still. It was maddening, but the pull toward him was certainly there as much as I didn't want it.

"Your friends and your mother like it here, Harmonia," he pointed out needlessly.

"Yes," I snapped. "Because you've made it so. You can't just steal them away and keep them. They have lives in the mortal world."

I found it odd that none of the three were asking any questions about their surroundings or the supernatural element that was around them. They had been abruptly thrust into it, yet they acted as if everything was normal, as though they had forgotten their mortal upbringings. They weren't even curious about my appearance- I was wearing clothing from my home on Olympus and I was covered in my husband's blood. I hadn't yet had time to wash it off. And none of them found that odd?

"Harmonia," Hades began smoothly, his voice like melted butter. "You must do what I wish or these three lovely ladies will no longer be welcome here with me. I'll have to send them away to Tartara. Do you want that?"

They immediately began protesting and crying at the thought of being separated from Hades, not at the thought of being sent to Tartara. I shook my head in wonderment. This was absolutely insane. Yet, on one level, I understood it. If his magnetism was hard for *me* to resist, it must be impossible for them. And they probably had no idea what Tartara even was. But I did.

"What do you want?" I growled.

"Oh, it's a decision you've had to make before, Chosen One. And you made it then. Let us see if you will choose the same now. You for them."

A rush of déjà vu washed over me. Yes, I had certainly been faced with this before, when the Fates had forced me to choose between my own life and those of everyone that I loved, including Cadmus. I had stood on the lip of a massive fire pit and had eventually decided to sacrifice myself. I exhaled a ragged sigh. I had even more to lose now. I had a daughter.

"You won't lose her," Hades replied to my thought. "She can stay with you. I don't ask for your life, I simply ask for you to stay here in the Underworld with me."

The darkness seemed to swirl around me as I weighed his demand. It was so much to think about that I could scarcely process it.

"And if I don't?" I murmured.

"Then Tartara will have three new prisoners," Hades answered smoothly and strangely without malice. "I don't wish to torture you, Harmonia. I simply know no other way to gain your cooperation.

"I need you to wake up now. Sneak outside of the palace and you will find someone waiting to bring you to me. Come alone. Do not wake Cadmus or anyone else. If you do, the consequences will be dire. I will not only send your mother and friends to Tartara, but I will be forced to take your daughter, as well. Don't force me to do that."

He studied me for a silent moment, his handsome face impassive as he waited. I struggled internally for a moment, but quickly came to the realization that I had no choice.

I nodded. "Fine. I will come to you and we will discuss this."

"Oh, I doubt there will be much discussion. But come to me. And these three women will be saved."

I opened my eyes. I was safely in bed with Cadmus and Raquel. But I wasn't truly safe, I knew that. And at the moment, neither were Jess, Jenn or my mother. I sighed and brushed a kiss across Raquel's brow. She was sleeping quietly, her face angelic in her slumber. I watched her for a moment, memorizing every plane of her face. I had no idea when I would see her again. I leaned over her and kissed Cadmus lightly on the cheek without waking him. In his sleep, he tightened his arm around us and a knot tightened in my throat. Quietly, I slipped from under his arm and out of bed.

"Mama?" A small voice called. "Where are you going?"

I startled and turned back. "Raquel, I thought you were asleep," I whispered, leaning back over the bed.

She shook her head. "I'm too excited to sleep." I brushed her hair away from her face.

"I'll be back in just a while, sweetpea," I murmured. "You stay here with daddy and keep him company, alright?"

She nodded trustingly and I swallowed hard as I bent to kiss her one more time before I turned and walked into the hall, working my way stealthily to the main floor of the palace.

Peeking out the back windows, I found everyone still dancing and laughing outside in the courtyard. I crept past the windows lining the terrace and out onto a side porch. I stopped abruptly when I found Eris sitting on the top step. Her dark hair was piled on her head and her white gown was spread around her.

She looked at me for a moment, but her gaze was not vindictive. It was just… matter-of-fact.

"I've been waiting for you," she murmured.

I returned her gaze and lifted my chin. It had seemed that treachery had found me once again. Would it never end?

# Chapter Thirteen

"I should have expected this from you," I hissed as I stepped down the wide stone steps after Eris. "What was I thinking in trusting you?"

Eris glanced over her shoulder at me as we quickly walked away from the palace. "Normally, you would be correct and entirely valid in your opinion of me. This time, however, I have had no choice. Hades has Alexi's soul now. He said that he will return it to us if I do this one thing."

"It's always 'one thing' with you, isn't it?" I asked wearily. "The Fates asked 'one thing' of you before- to bewitch Cadmus and kidnap him to the Spiritlands. You happily did that, didn't you?"

"Are we back to that?" she snapped. "They promised to return my immortality. Surely you can understand why I took that deal!"

I tried to block the unwanted images of Cadmus and Eris locked in an embrace. She had bewitched him and given him a love potion to make him think that he was in love with her. She had taken him back to her home in the Spiritlands in order to lure Aphrodite and me there. It had worked and Eris had taken quite a lot of enjoyment in taunting me with that situation. It was hard to forget but I shook the memories away now. Now wasn't the time to dwell on the past.

"No. I probably will never forgive you for that. But I suppose that I can somewhat understand your actions today," I admitted gruffly. "I, too, would do anything for those that I love. I find that I cannot hold it against you."

Eris looked strangely vulnerable for a moment and I wondered, just briefly, if she did possess a conscience after all. But she quickly masked it and continued walking briskly. I followed behind her and we fell into silence, but it wasn't long until we came to a Lotus tree.

An owl was perched on the lowest limb and I would almost swear that it was the same owl that I saw next to the Necromanteion. I studied it and it looked back at me with unblinking amber eyes. It had to be the same. Eris held out her hand and the owl extended a clenched claw, dropping two small bright pink blossoms onto her palm. She held one out to me and put the other in her mouth.

"No, don't!" I cried, reaching out to stop her, but it was too late. She was already chewing.

"Eris, what have you done? You know that you cannot leave here now."

She stared at me calmly.

"What I know is that things are very muddled right now. It is difficult to say who will wind up on top. And is there really a 'top'? I find, as time goes on, that things are rarely what they seem and power is a very fluid and finicky thing. Eating these is the only way to quickly arrive at Hades' palace, a place where we both need to be. If Zeus comes to his senses, perhaps he will provide a way for us to return. If not, perhaps Hades will be good to us." She shrugged her thin shoulders and then swallowed.

I stared at her in apprehension. Her words were uncharacteristically wise. She was right. We had no idea who would end up in control when all was said and done. In the meantime, we had to do what we needed to do in order to take care of ourselves. I reached out a shaking hand and took the flower. Chewing it, I damned myself to an eternal existence in the Underworld. My only hope now was that someone took mercy on me and set me free. I swallowed. But it was what I had to do. And as a mother, I would do it again and again and again in order to secure Raquel's safety.

Eris looked at me and nodded. "Ready?" She grasped my hand and we were gone.

Before I knew it, we were standing in front of Hades' imposing palace. My head whirled just a bit from the instantaneous travel, but after just a moment, I felt back to normal. I felt just like any other person would who was walking to their eternal damnation: Numb.

The drawbridge lowered and the guards nodded to us. Clearly, we were expected. We quickly entered, stepping into the entryway and found Hades waiting.

"Ladies," he nodded. I stared at him in return. He might think that he wanted to keep me for all of eternity, but I was not going to make it pleasant. "Welcome back."

He snapped his fingers and a hunchbacked undead servant appeared.

"Yes, sir?" the servant asked.

"Bring Alexi," Hades demanded.

I stared at him dumbfounded. "How did you get him so fast? He was in Zeus' palace when I left."

Hades smiled. "No, he wasn't. He was in Zeus' palace when you retired for a nap. Now he is here."

He offered no explanation and I found that I really didn't care to know how he had retrieved Alexi so quickly. Within minutes, the servant had returned with him. As always, Alexi was cold and unemotional. I knew now that it was because his soul was gone. I hadn't known that when I had first met him- when he had shown up in my bedroom in the mortal world to take me to the Spiritlands for the Fates. I had just thought he was a jerk.

He stood before me now, his arms limply at his sides, his eyes straight ahead. He was handsome in a very pale way. He wasn't my personal cup of tea, but Eris was staring at him with hearts in her eyes. I couldn't believe that I had never noticed that before, either. I briefly wondered how long it had been going on before Hades moved to a corner of the room.

The Box of Souls sat on a marble pedestal. I almost cried out, but restrained myself. How had Hades gotten it from the Keres? But just as soon as I wondered, the answer came to me. Obviously,

Alecto had somehow finagled it. I found that once again, I didn't want to know the details.

Hades opened the lid and simply reached into the box. Within a second, he had withdrawn his hand and closed the box once again, turning around to face us.

"You realize the price?" he asked Eris.

She nodded stoically, without saying a word.

"You are bound to me for eternity," Hades said. "You belong to me now."

Eris nodded once more, one short determined nod. I didn't bother to protest or try to intervene. I knew what it was like to trade yourself for someone else. I knew her mind would not be swayed. I had to admit, I respected her for her decision. She was putting someone above herself, something I never thought I would see.

"Very well," Hades said pleasantly. "We have a deal."

He extended his hand and opened his fingers, blowing a puff of air in that direction. A shimmery cloud formed in front of us and sailed directly toward Alexi. He automatically opened his mouth and then stiffened as the cloud filled him up. He was rigid and silent for a moment while color quickly flooded his cheeks. The change was immediate and obvious.

Alexi looked around in confusion for a moment before he was able to compose himself. The first expression to cross his face was a perplexed one. And then relief as he saw Eris.

"Eris?" he breathed.

She flew into his arms in record time and I had the sudden urge to cry. Somehow, my arch nemesis had managed to procure a deal that would keep she and her beloved together for eternity. It didn't matter to them that they belonged to Hades now- they would face that together. I felt an overwhelming rush of jealousy. I didn't have that anymore. I had to leave my soul mate in order to protect my family. It was the story of my life.

"Now, then," Hades said pleasantly. "You may return to the Spiritlands. You will be more useful there than here right now."

"The Spiritlands?" Eris repeated uncertainly. Hades nodded.

"Yes," he confirmed. "Sometimes it is very useful to me to have people on the outside. You will assist me greatly in the future, I can feel it."

Eris' shoulders dropped just a bit and I saw the corners of Hades' mouth curl slightly.

"It will be fine, Eris," he soothed. "I protect my own. Now, go."

He waved his hand and Eris and Alexi were gone. I was left alone in the foyer with the god of the Underworld. He assessed my mood from where he stood, his dark head cocked thoughtfully.

"And here you are," he murmured, moving smoothly to my side. Lifting one slender hand, he stroked the side of my face. I struggled to not flinch. "You have done the right thing," he assured me. "You will be happy here."

"Will I?" I asked sharply. "I've had to leave my family."

"We'll discuss that over dinner," he replied, offering me his arm. "Now that you can eat here, I have had a feast prepared in your honor. I'll allow you to retire to your rooms to freshen up. You'll find fresh clothing for you on your bed."

He had laid out clothing for me? Strange. I shook my head, but knew that there was nothing I could do but comply. He led me to a suite of rooms, but instead of leaving me, he followed me in. I turned to him in surprise.

"Why are you staying?"

"Because I'm not ready to leave you yet," he replied smoothly. His expression was almost eager and the fact that we were alone together in a bedroom slammed into me. I backed away.

"I will never give myself to you willingly," I promised.

"We'll see," he murmured, sliding back up next to me. "Never is a very long time and I'm very patient. But for now, I only wanted to show you something. Come look."

He moved to one corner of the elaborate suite and pulled a velvet curtain away from a long mirror. It stood at least seven feet tall and was framed in wrought gold.

"Show me Raquel," he demanded. Instantly, the sparkling mirror shimmered and I could see inside Zeus' palace, where

Raquel and Cadmus were still peacefully sleeping. They had no idea yet that I was even gone. I felt a rush of relief. Even though it was inevitable, I wanted to put off their heartache for just a bit longer.

"Is this what you meant when you said that I could remain with her?" I asked. "Because that wasn't quite what I had in mind."

He smiled gently. "There are a couple of options," he answered. "And we'll discuss them at dinner. First, you should wash. Then you must get dressed." He waved his hand toward the bed and I found a gorgeous jade green crushed-velvet gown there. It was exactly the color of my eyes. "Go ahead. Don't be shy," he added.

"You want me to get dressed… while you are here watching?" I was incredulous. He smiled again and stepped back to sit on a chair in the corner. He was almost entirely concealed by the shadows, yet every inch of my body felt his presence.

"Go ahead," he instructed softly. "I'm harmless. Pretend I am not even here. I know you will look lovely in this gown. I selected it myself. I cannot wait to see it on you."

"I'm not washing," I said firmly. "It's my husband's blood. If you don't like it, don't look at me."

A low chuckle came from the corner. "I'm the god of the Underworld," he said. "Do you think the sight of blood bothers me?"

I sighed and turned to the gown. It was silly to refuse to wash, but as long as Cadmus' blood was still smeared on me, then I felt as though he was still here with me, in a strange way.

The shadows covered Hades' face, so I tried to pretend that he wasn't here with me. Turning my back to him, I lowered my thigh-length tunic and allowed it to drop to my ankles. I stepped out of it and reached for the gown, but Hades voice murmured into my ear from directly behind me. He had moved so quietly that I didn't even hear him.

"Allow me," he breathed. He held out the gown and I moved away from him.

"I'll never allow you to touch me," I snarled. "I'm a married woman. My heart belongs to Cadmus."

"Trust me, I'll never touch you against your will," he promised. "I'm simply going to help you with this gown. The buttons are complicated."

I eyed him for a moment and then sighed, stepping into the gown and pulling it up as quickly as I could, covering my naked body. He fastened the buttons that lined my back, standing so close that I could feel his warm breath on my neck. Regardless of my protests that I would never let him touch me, my body longed for it. It was an effect that I couldn't control and I couldn't ignore. My nerve endings were on fire where he touched and I ached to lean closer to him. I hated it. But I couldn't help it.

He brought his lips to the side of my bare neck and brushed them softly along my skin. Without meaning to, I whimpered and then silently cursed myself. I didn't want him to know the effect he had on me. Steeling myself, I focused on Cadmus' face in my mind, trying desperately to ignore Hades' powerful charm.

*Block it out, block it out,* I chanted silently.

I had forgotten, however, that Hades could read my thoughts and I felt him smile against my neck.

"Just as I thought," he said softly. "You're exquisite. I'll leave you now to finish."

He was gone and I didn't even hear the door close behind him. Letting my breath exhale in a rush, I turned to the mirror on the vanity. The gown was becoming. It was strapless and hugged my form, with a slit on one side all the way to my hip. My husband's blood was still smeared on my arms and my cheek and I felt a tiny bit of satisfaction. Maybe it would act as a reminder to Hades that I was a married woman. Not that it mattered to him.

On the vanity counter, I saw a glittering emerald necklace, chunky and elaborate. I smirked.

*Nice try, Hades,* I thought.

I hoped that he was listening to my thoughts right now. There was no way that I was removing my bloodstone and replacing it with any other necklace. No way in… well, Hades.

I looked into the magic mirror one more time before leaving and found my husband and daughter still sleeping. I traced the outlines of their faces on the glass, sadness welling up in my heart. Was this really going to be my future? I would forever be damned to watching them from a mirror? I swallowed a lump in my throat and turned away, leaving my new bedchambers for dinner.

When I arrived in the dining room, I found Hades already seated at one end of the table. Persephone was at the other end, radiant in a canary yellow satin gown. Bright yellow sapphires adorned her hair and her neck. She didn't look pleased to see me, not that I could blame her.

"I'm sorry, Persephone," I told her quietly. "I do not wish to be here."

She nodded. "I'm sure," she acknowledged. "But it doesn't change the fact that you are."

I ignored that and walked to the only other place setting at the long table. I was situated directly between Persephone and Hades. Before I knew it, he was behind me, sliding out my chair like a perfect gentleman. I sighed again and was seated. This might possibly be the strangest position I had ever been in. I was sitting directly in the middle of a husband and wife. The husband wanted to sleep with me- to possess me- and the wife had full knowledge of that and to top it off, they loved each other deeply. What an odd marriage.

Hades snapped his fingers and servants began bringing in the courses of our meal. Having not eaten in days, I was starving and practically inhaled my food. Each bite was delicious and my goblet was kept full of ice cold nectar. I tried to talk about my situation, but Hades shushed me.

"You need to eat," he observed. "We'll speak in a while."

It was true- while I desperately wanted to nail down the details of this deal with Hades, I was insanely hungry. I put another bite in my mouth, then another. Finally, we finished up dessert and it was time to talk.

"Now, back to your issue of family," Hades began. I was pleasantly full and the nectar had replenished my strength. I could feel my cheeks flushing from its effects, just as a mortal's would flush with too much wine.

"You mentioned something about options?" I asked casually, staring at him in the eye. His twinkled happily. I was certain that whatever they were, the options were all to his benefit.

"Yes," he confirmed. "You have a couple. First, you may stay in this palace with me while Raquel and Cadmus continue to stay in the Isles of the Blessed. This would not be a bad option, Chosen One. The isles are filled with every luxury and everything that they could possibly ever want or desire. It is truly a paradise. And you will, of course, retain your magic mirror. You can see them at any given time."

"And my second option?" I tried to ensure that my voice didn't waver, but it was difficult. The thought of never being with my family again was soul-shattering.

"Your second option is to bring them here, to reside with us here in the palace. They will be here with you, and they will have freedom to come and go as they please, roaming anywhere in the Underworld that they wish."

"And me?" I asked quietly.

"You will be confined to the palace grounds," Hades answered. "It is your energy that I find exquisite. I want you near me at all times."

At the other end of the table, Persephone slammed down her goblet, but she remained silent. I glanced in her direction and found her glaring angrily at her husband. He remained unfazed, waiting for my answer.

"Why can't they return to the Spiritlands?" I asked. "Why must they remain here at all?"

"Because that simply isn't an option," he replied firmly. "But the Isles are a paradise, even more so than the Spiritlands. They are better off there, anyway."

"In your opinion," I added. He smiled.

"My opinion is the only one that matters here."

Unfortunately, I knew that he was right. I was completely at his mercy. And I didn't want my family to be under his thumb on a daily basis. I didn't want my daughter anywhere near him. He nodded.

"Excellent choice," he approved. "They shall stay in the Isles."

My heart broke at his words, but I didn't say a word. It was necessary. I had to protect them, no matter the cost.

"And what of my mortal mother and my friends?" I asked.

He smiled. "I will return them post-haste to their mortal lives. I didn't really need them here, I simply needed them to bring you here."

"But what of their memories from here?" I asked, troubled. "They will forever be haunted by this."

"No," he answered. "They won't be. I shall simply erase those memories. They will have no recollection of this time, whatsoever. It is very easy, really."

A thought occurred to me and I hesitantly wondered if I should ask. Hades saved me from my unease.

"Of course," he answered my thoughts. "That is actually a very considerate idea. I can certainly erase you from their memories, as well. I can eliminate all traces of Macy Lockhart's existence in the mortal world. That might be the most humane thing to do in this situation, don't you agree?"

I nodded numbly. I hated it. I would miss my mother and Jess and Jenn… but I couldn't live with the thought that they were missing me, too. It would be better if I never existed to them at all.

"Consider it done," Hades concluded. I nodded silently, willing myself not to cry.

We finished our after-dinner drinks in silence and I excused myself to my rooms. Looking around, I studied my new quarters. They were elaborate and lavish. Hades had spared no expense, but I didn't care. The bed was large and soft, encased in a billowing canopy and sheer side panels. Fluffy pillows were piled on top and I threw myself onto them, sobbing into them quietly. In all my mortal lives, I had never known such pain as this. It filled me up and I couldn't think past it. So, I cried. It was the only thing I could think of to do.

I cried for at least an hour and when my heaving sobs finally subsided, I lay spent for a moment longer before I sat up, reaching a shaking hand up to smooth my hair. I glanced at the magic mirror. Did I want to see? I knew by now, they had to know that I was gone. Did I really want to see that?

No, I didn't. I couldn't stand to see Cadmus in pain or see the look on Raquel's face. I couldn't imagine what she would feel. She had only just discovered that I was her mother and to have me snatched away now, it would have to be devastating for such a little girl. I truly hoped that Aphrodite would swoop in and provide all of the motherly things that Cadmus wouldn't be able to provide. He was a glorious father, but children needed a mother's touch in some things.

Standing up, I re-covered the mirror with a velvet drape. I would look again sometime in the near future, but I couldn't handle it today. My heart was just too fragile.

Straightening my clothes, I left my rooms to explore the palace. I would do anything to occupy my mind so that I didn't focus on how on my own devastation.

My suite was apparently in a wing dedicated to bedrooms. It was quiet and tranquil during the day with the halls lit softly. I followed the winding corridors out until I emerged in a great room. Books lined the walls, from floor to ceiling and I found Persephone seated by a raging fire, a book in her hands. She wasn't reading it, however. She was staring absently into the flames.

"I've heard that you can control the Phoenix," she murmured, without looking up. I had no idea how she knew it was me and I didn't ask. I quietly crossed the room and seated myself in the chair opposing her.

"Yes," I answered simply. The fire felt wonderfully warm and quickly made me sleepy. The emotions of the day had drained me and I closed my eyes, soaking in the warmth.

"It must be exquisite to be in control of so much power," she replied. I felt her eyes on my face, but I didn't open my own. I was suddenly very, very weary.

"Not particularly," I answered. "I don't even know how I do it sometimes. It just happens."

"That is because the bird is in tune with you," she mused. "I have a book here somewhere about the Phoenix. You are welcome to read it. In fact, you are welcome to use anything that you find here…except for my husband."

My eyes snapped open.

"I don't wish to use your husband," I snapped. "I don't want anything to do with him and I don't want to be here at all. I want to be with my own husband and my daughter and the rest of my family."

"Nevertheless," she continued. "I'm very possessive and when Hades wants something, he can be very persistent and patient. Don't think that I don't know what kind of effect he has on women. In fact, he has the same effect on men- it just manifests itself differently. People, male or female, usually endeavor to please him. Something about him is so… delicious."

"I don't find it delicious," I confided. "I find it disturbing. I don't wish to have any feelings about him at all."

"But you will," she sighed. "Particularly now that you are living here with us. Resist it as much as you would like, but I am sure it is bound to happen. Unless Hades loses interest. That could always happen."

I shook my head. "Just remember… I don't want your husband. I only want my own."

"But your own is not here. And you will be here a very long time, away from Cadmus. You can remember that."

She rose from her seat and took two steps to stand next to me. Bending, she kissed a cool kiss on my cheek. She smelled vaguely of oriental spices.

"It will be nice to have female company," she murmured. "I'm sorry that this has happened to you, Harmonia. You are a sweet girl. But take comfort knowing this: I didn't like the Underworld at first, either. But it has become my home and I am happy here. So you shall be, too."

Her long skirts rustled as she glided from the room and I found myself staring at the fire in the same exact way she had been doing when I had found her. The flames were warm and mesmerizing, a good way to allow my overwhelmed mind to rest. I stared into them until the warmth lulled me to sleep.

Immediately, Cadmus faced me, his face drawn and anxious. He was clearly beside himself, as I knew he would be.

"Where are you?" he demanded. "I'll come to you, just tell me where."

My heart automatically lurched hopefully, but I tampered it back down. He couldn't help me. No matter how strong of a warrior he was, he couldn't help me now.

"You can't," I answered sadly. "I am with Hades and you can't come here. You can't help me. I'm sorry, Cadmus. I had to come. Hades threatened everyone that I know and love. He brought my mother here, and Jess and Jenn… I had to exchange myself for them. And if I refused, he would've come for you and Raquel. This was the only way."

"There is never only *one way,*" he admonished me painfully. "You should have come to me and we would have figured something out. Something feasible. Your parents are beside themselves and Raquel…" his voice trailed off. I nodded sadly.

"I know. Please tell her that I love her and I'll always love her. Everything that I do is for the two of you. Please believe that."

"I do," he said. "I believe you, of course I do. I just know there has to be another way."

His handsome bronzed face was tormented and he paced to and fro as he spoke. With each step, his taut muscles flexed and he reminded me of a caged lion.

"I will think of something, wife. I will not leave you there."

"You have to," I whispered, leaning up to kiss him. His lips were warm and soft and I wanted to stay in his arms forever, even if it was only in a dream. "I love you, Cadmus."

I forced myself awake. I couldn't stand the pain on my husband's face for one more second. It was killing me. I stood from the chair and retreated back to my rooms, lying on my side in the giant soft bed. It was strange, sleeping alone again without Cadmus at my side. I gritted my teeth and stayed awake as long as I could. I wanted to make sure that Cadmus wouldn't be waiting for me in my dreams again. As much as I wanted to see him, seeing him this way was unbearable.

# Chapter Fourteen

No one could say that I didn't go through the motions. I went to sleep, I ate with Persephone and Hades, I went for walks in the gardens, I read books in the library. But my heart was dead. Day by day, I forced myself to become number and number, until finally I felt like a living, breathing, piece of wood.

It was the only way I could survive it.

Being away from those that I loved was torturous, an existence that I wouldn't wish on anyone. I could even forgive Eris for defecting to Hades' side, because he had given her back Alexi. I knew the feeling now- I would do anything to get my family back. I thought about begging Hades, to see if there was anything at all that I could do to pay for my own freedom. It was a long shot, though, so I mulled on it for quite a while. I didn't want to ask, only to be shot down. It would be a crushing blow.

One evening, as Hades and I sat by the fire in the crushed velvet armchairs, I looked up from the book that I was reading.

"Hades," I began uncertainly. "Is there anything at all that I can do to persuade you to let me go? It is killing me inside to be away from my family. I feel as though I am dying slowly."

He looked up from his own book and studied me thoughtfully. With his dark gaze glued to mine, he closed his book slowly and rose from his chair, kneeling in front of me. Taking my hands, he whispered.

"There is one thing."

"What is it?" I cried. "I'll do anything. Please. I promise you, I'll do anything."

He smiled and brushed the hair away from my face gently. "Anything?"

I nodded silently although the expression on his handsome face caused my stomach to sink.

"I want you," he murmured, leaning up to kiss the side of my neck. His lips grazed my skin ever so softly, enough to leave a trail of goose bumps. "And not just once. That would never be enough. I want you for one night a year for the rest of eternity."

I fell silent as I listened to the beat of my own heart. It throbbed against my ribcage loudly, echoing in the room.

"What do you think of my terms?" he asked, sliding his thumb along my bottom lip. I wavered. I had never felt so desperate in my life. But to expect Cadmus to live with that—to return here to the palace for one night a year… and heaven only knew what perverted things Hades might do to me. I would almost rather die.

I shook my head slowly. "I can't," I whispered.

He was disappointed, I could see it on his face. But he didn't say so. Instead, he simply stood and returned to his chair, re-opening his book.

"The offer stands," he said as he casually went back to reading. I squeezed my eyes closed and forced away the pain. I would do anything. But that.

* * *

Days turned into weeks.

I could never say that that either Persephone or Hades were cruel to me or even unpleasant. It wasn't true. In fact, it was the opposite. They were kind and welcoming. But each day was more painful for me than the last because nothing changed the fact that I was a prisoner.

I realized more than ever that I was a person who thrived on loving relationships. I needed them. I overheard Hades and Persephone whispering in the hall one day.

"She is wilting," Persephone said anxiously. "I can see it more and more every day. She eats, she drinks nectar, yet she grows weaker. I don't know what to do."

"Being away from her family seems to drain her," Hades observed. "Let us give her time. Surely she will grow accustomed to being here and she will rally."

"But her light grows faint," Persephone replied. "I can sense it around her and the energy around the palace that she brought with her is fading. Surely you can see that."

"I can," Hades admitted. "But she is strong. She has always recovered, no matter what life has thrown at her. I am certain this will be no different."

*Don't be so certain,* I thought.

At dinner that evening, Hades casually asked me if I had seen my family through the mirror recently.

"No," I admitted limply, shoving my food around on my plate. "I cannot bring myself to do it."

"But you should," Hades encouraged me. "If you but see them, you will feel much better. I am certain."

"Don't be," I answered sharply. "You've taken them from me. Don't feel that you can force me to watch them from here. It is too heartbreaking. It will only make things worse."

"Well, I'll leave that to you," he replied quickly. "You know what you need more than anyone."

"I need my family," I answered quietly.

"Well, you can't have them!" he thundered, pushing away from the table and throwing his chair across the room. It smashed into a shelf of crystal vases, shattering them. "You know the price!"

He stormed from the room without looking back. I was left staring after him. It was the first time I had ever seen him lose his temper. He was always carefully composed.

"You must recover," Persephone told me quietly. "You will fade away, Harmonia."

"No, I will not," I snapped. "No one dies of a broken heart. Those are just romantic stories. But trust me, it isn't romantic at all if it is happening to you."

"Take him up on his bargain," she suggested. "It will end this. You will be returned to them and Hades will be happy."

I looked at her, appalled. "This, coming from his wife?"

She shook her head. "I will always be the most important to him. That is what matters. I wish to see him happy and I hate seeing you wasting away. Pay his price."

She looked at me sadly before she continued eating and we finished our meal in silence.

After I returned to my rooms, I sat limply on my bed for what seemed like hours before I finally uncovered the mirror.

"Show me my family," I whispered hesitantly. Immediately, I saw Raquel and Aphrodite on a beach. Raquel was flying a bright red kite with yellow bows on the string and she left little footprints in the sand as she ran. Aphrodite followed behind her, as beautiful and perfect as always. But her face was sad as she watched my daughter.

I kept watching as Raquel splashed into the surf, but was surprised to see Aphrodite look around warily. Confusion was etched on her face and she appeared to search for someone. And then she met my gaze through the mirror. She sensed my presence, I realized with a start.

"Be patient, Harmonia," she whispered. "We love you and we are doing all that we can. Your sadness is affecting the mortal world, unhappiness has descended upon it like a fog. We are trying to reason with Zeus, to show him that he is truly needed to right these wrongs or everyone will suffer. Hang on, my sweet. We are coming."

I knew she couldn't see me, but I nodded anyway as tears filled my eyes. My sadness was affecting the mortal world? I guessed it made sense. I was the goddess of peace and contentment. If my positive energy faded, then it made sense that the world would suffer. If that was the case… then what would happen if I gave up trying? What if I gave in to my depression? Would it affect the mortal world in a way that would truly make Zeus see that he needed to return? Because if he returned, perhaps he could save us all.

It was worth a try.

And honestly, it wasn't difficult. I was so very tired. The weight of the world had rested upon my shoulders for more times than I could count. It was time to set that weight down. I climbed into bed and pulled the covers up to my chin, closing my eyes.

The darkness was comforting. Soft and warm like a favorite blanket, it closed around me and lingered. I drifted down, down, down, until I felt as though I were floating. Either in a body of water or midair—I floated away from reality. My pain and sorrow came with me and I didn't fight it. I dwelled in it.

At some point, maybe hours or maybe days later, I heard vague voices around me, distant and quiet, as though someone was speaking through a veil.

"Her despair is turning the world black," a voice whispered. "We must do something, Hades."

"There is nothing to do," he answered. "She must return to herself. That is the only way."

"Return her to her family," a voice suggested. Persephone? "That is a way."

"Unthinkable!" he roared. "What message would that send?"

"It would send the message that you care what happens outside of the Underworld!"

I stopped listening. My plan was working. My depression was affecting the world. I felt sorry for the mortal world, sorry for the part I was playing in making them unhappy. But it was the only thing I could think of that might help.

So I drifted further away.

Through the black mists surrounding me, I heard voices sometimes, not voices standing next to my body, but voices echoing in my head.

Cadmus' husky whisper, "I love you. Please hold on."

Aphrodite murmured, "Harmonia, all will be fine. Continue with what you are doing. It is working. We love you."

"We love you."

"We love you."

Those words echoed in my black thoughts and I pushed them away. I couldn't dwell on positive things- I had to keep my energy black. It was against my nature and it was difficult, but I found that if I focused, I could do it.

At one point, I heard Ares. "You are strong, daughter. We love you."

I knew I had to move away from the loving thoughts- past the point where I could hear them. I pushed myself further away, drifting on the depression. My surroundings turned blacker. Days passed.

Then weeks.

Time was nothing to me. It ran together like water. I had finally managed a way to suspend myself away from reality and I knew that I was in a strange, hypnotic state. I had tricked my own mind. It was unfathomable. But in my desperation, I had done it.

And then came his voice. The only voice that had mattered for thousands of years.

"We're coming."

I withdrew from the darkness in an instant, my eyes popping open.

Persephone sat by my bed, reading quietly. As I stirred, her eyes flew to my face.

"You're back," she breathed. "I must get Hades."

I reached out a weak arm. Lying motionless in a bed had taken a toll.

"Don't," I pleaded in a whisper. "I need to get dressed. Please. Can you help me?"

She took one look at my face and relented.

"Of course," she said kindly. "We can get Hades afterward. Come, let me help you up."

She put her arms behind me and helped me sit. The room spun in a whirl, but after a moment, it stilled.

"How long have I been sleeping?" I asked.

"Two months," she answered grimly. "You have no idea of the ramifications. Your sadness has affected the world."

I didn't tell her that I knew. I simply allowed her to help me into a loose tunic and sat calmly while she brushed my hair and braided it over my shoulder.

"I'm glad that you have returned to us," she said quietly. "I was worried about you. I have never seen such a thing."

"Neither have I," I whispered. And I hoped to never again. It had left me feeling incredibly weak, absolutely drained of energy. I reached up and grasped my bloodstone. It wasn't helping me now.

"If it helps, your family has been here several times," she offered quietly. "Ares, Aphrodite and Cadmus. They came several times to see you, but the guards wouldn't let them pass."

"Was anyone hurt?" I asked quickly. She shook her head.

"No."

Before I could say anything else, an amazingly loud bellow rang in my ears and vibrated the walls of the palace.

"HADES!"

It was so loud that it left my ears ringing.

Persephone and I stared at each other in alarm, before I got shakily to my feet. I remembered Cadmus' words. *We're coming.*

They were here.

"We should go," I suggested. I took her arm and we hurried as fast as we could to the main floor of the palace. With each step, I felt stronger and by the time we arrived in the foyer, I was standing on my own. We arrived at the same time as Hades.

"Hades!" The voice resounded again and this time, I knew in my heart it was Zeus. He had come after all. Joy flooded my heart. He was here. "Open the gates!"

Hades sucked on his lip for a moment and then nodded, motioning to a guard. The guard disappeared outside and within moments, the drawbridge was lowered. I rushed to the window. The Olympians stood outside, along with my husband. They had truly come. It was a sight to behold.

Zeus stood in the front and he held Hades' helm of darkness. His eyes flashed silver and were fierce and proud. He had returned to himself, I could see it in his expression. I had never felt so relieved.

On each of his sides, stood Hera and Poseidon. Lined up in a row were Demeter, Athena, Dionysus, Apollo, Artemis, Hermes, Ares and Aphrodite. On the far end was Hephaestus. They had apparently summoned him from the Spiritlands. On the other side, stood my husband, flanked by Hecate and Annen.

And my heart started beating again. It suddenly felt as though it had been silent the entire time I had been separated from Cadmus. But now that he was here, I could breathe again. He was tall and beautiful, gazing fiercely at the palace…ready to fight for me. Behind him, stood Ortrera and her warriors. Every single face was fierce and determined. A flicker lit inside of me and I dared to let myself hope.

Maybe, just maybe.

"Come outside!" Zeus thundered. "Or I will take apart your palace brick by brick."

Hades sighed, then straightened his shoulders. Stepping forward, he flung open the doors.

Cadmus' gaze fixed on mine and he grinned a slow grin. *I'm coming,* he mouthed. I smiled back. *It's about time,* I mouthed back. He grinned wider.

"What is the meaning of this?" Hades asked the Olympians. "I thought you were happy on the Isles. You seemed to be the last time I visited."

"You had us deluded, brother," Zeus admonished. "But no more. We have seen what you have done to the world. Unrest plagues the mortal world, all because you have separated the goddess of contentment from those that she loves. Until she is happy once more, discontent will plague the earth. Yet, you did not act. You are not the god to rule the world, Hades. You may keep the Underworld, but I am taking back the rest."

Hades face clouded over.

"You think?" he growled. "You can do nothing, *brother.* You are condemned to stay here because you allowed yourself to be deceived. You have eaten here, so here you shall stay. Have you forgotten that small fact?"

Zeus smiled, a smile full of satisfaction and arrogance.

"There is one small thing that I should point out." His gaze shifted to me. "Harmonia, dear. Step forward."

Hades eyed me from his periphery. "Stay," he growled to me.

"She is still on the palace grounds," Zeus said. "She is not breaking her word."

Frustration washed across Hades face. It was true. I was still on palace grounds, as agreed. I stepped forward.

"Closer," Zeus instructed. I took a few more steps and he met me in the middle, wrapping his arm around my shoulders.

"Do you see the pendant hanging around her neck?" Zeus inquired politely. Hades scowled.

"Of course, I see her bloodstone. Everyone knows of it. It brings her bad fortune."

Zeus nodded. "Yes. I allowed Hephaestus to curse it so that no one else would want it. That way, it has always remained safe with Harmonia."

Hades face grew instantly wary.

"Do you know why, brother?" Zeus asked, still polite.

Hades shook his head, clearly annoyed.

"Because it contains my blood," Zeus explained, as though that cleared up the confusion. "I'm sure you are aware of the caveat… if any part of me remains in the Underworld, the rest of me is free to leave. A small vial of my blood is concealed in the center of the bloodstone. It is my key to freedom from your treachery."

"No!" Hades cried. "That is impossible."

"Oh, yes," Zeus confirmed, shaking his large head. "Did you think that you are the only cunning one in our family? I outsmarted you. My plan has taken years to unfold, but here we are. The key is now in my hands."

With his words, he lifted the bloodstone from around my neck and gripped it tightly.

"As long as this bloodstone remains here in the Underworld, you cannot keep me here," Zeus said needlessly. "I will return to Olympus."

"Not Harmonia," Hades snapped. "That may hold true for you, but Harmonia has eaten here, so here she shall remain. The others, also. Everyone but you shall remain."

"Oh, Hades," Zeus shook his head. "That isn't true. Everyone shall leave. And do you know why? Because I know you want your helm back. Isn't that true?"

There was a long pregnant pause. Of course Hades wanted his helm back. He needed it. Without it, he couldn't access his full potential in the Underworld. The realization was written on his face.

"I will give you back your helm, in exchange for everyone's freedom," Zeus bargained. "You know it is not an option. You must have it. So, I'll give it to you and we'll return to Olympus. We'll let bygones be bygones and we'll return to how we were before. Or, we can do it the hard way, if you prefer. I can retrieve my sword and return here to face you head to head."

The air was thick and tense. Hades' displeasure was evident, his frustration palpable. But Zeus was right. There was no other choice that Hades could make. We all waited in anticipation to hear him admit it.

"Fine," he snapped. "We have a deal."

We all exhaled sighs of relief. Joy flooded through me and my knees grew weak as I bounded down the line of gods into my husband's arms. I wrapped my arms around his neck and pulled him down to kiss me. He had never tasted so good. Just being near him fed my spirit and I grew visibly stronger immediately. He held me tight and I inhaled him, his outdoorsy, Cadmus smell and I smiled.

"Don't be so happy quite yet, Harmonia," Hades said smoothly. "We have one minor thing left to discuss."

"And what would that be?" I asked. I wasn't worried now. If we were all free and I was back with my family, there was nothing else Hades could do to me that would matter.

"There's the little matter of your daughter's soul," Hades purred.

"My daughter's soul?" I asked in confusion. "What of it?"

"Well, I hate to bring this up during such a joyful time for you, but your daughter cannot leave. Only the living can leave. The dead must remain in the Underworld."

# Chapter Fifteen

"The dead?" I gasped. "Raquel's not… she's not…"

"Oh, I beg to differ," Hades replied. "She most certainly is not alive. Would you like to know why she is dead?"

I nodded, my heart frozen in my chest. It was true, that here in the Underworld, it was almost impossible to tell the difference between the living and the dead. And she hadn't slept once since we had found her. But surely… surely she was not dead. I waited stiffly to hear Hades' explanation.

"Because, you see, you were pregnant with her when you were in mortal form in Camelot. Your life there would have ended in childbirth and you both would have died. But the Fates saw fit to intervene. They thought that a new child brought into the mix would provide hours and hours of entertainment, so they saved her.

"When Hecate turned back the Fates' manipulations, it interfered with your daughter's life. It was as if the Fates had never interfered. Your daughter died and came here to the Underworld. There's nothing you can do."

There was a collective gasp and I flew to Zeus' side.

"Please, there must be something you can do. Can you repair what Hecate did? Can you fix it? Please!" I begged him as I grasped his large, wrinkled hand. Zeus stared at me sadly.

"Harmonia, it might be possible, but I should explain something. Think of fate like a magnificent tapestry. Many, many things are interwoven, each life a separate string. If one string is disturbed, it affects those around it. If I re-weave your daughter's string, it could have dire consequences for the strings around hers."

Panic rose in my throat, so much so that I could taste it.

"I care not!" I cried anxiously. "I only care for my daughter. Please. Save her."

"I think you might care if I told you which strings were next to hers, one in particular. Hecate has told me of Empusa's plight and Hecate has also begged me to intercede on Empusa's behalf.

"The problem is that their strings are next to each other. I cannot change them both. I can only alter one. To try to change both of them would likely destroy them both."

Another collective gasp and my gaze met Hecate's. Our daughters were both in grave danger and only one could come out intact.

"Only one?" Hecate asked. But we both already knew the answer.

"Only one," Zeus confirmed. "I can secure Empusa's freedom from the Underworld or I can give Raquel back her life. It is a sad choice, but unfortunately, it is reality. I cannot see a way around it."

If Zeus couldn't, then no one could. We all knew that.

"If I may be so bold," Hades interjected. "I might have a satisfactory idea."

"I doubt it," I muttered, glowering at him.

"Bear with me," he continued. "Allow Zeus to assist Empusa. I will go along with that willingly, not offering a fight at all, even though I would much rather have Empusa in the Underworld than Mormo's black soul. In return, I will allow the three of you- you, Cadmus and your daughter- to remain in the Isles of the Blessed. You can have full access to every level of the Underworld that you wish with no restrictions. You have seen yourself how happy the Olympians were there. You will be together with your family, the mortal world wouldn't have to suffer your pain and you can live in paradise for all of eternity."

You could have heard a pin drop around us. It was utterly silent as everyone thought about this offer. It seemed almost unconscionable to give up on my daughter now- to fold without even fighting. But then, there was another daughter on the line, too.

She just didn't happen to be my own… and she had taken very good care of my daughter when Raquel had been scared and alone.

I swallowed hard. It wouldn't really be giving up on my daughter. She was dead- she was meant to be here. What it would be… would be giving up on my own life in the Spiritlands. It would simply mean that I was choosing her over me. We'd be together and wasn't that the most important thing?

"Don't do it," Hecate said. "Your decision would be final. I could perhaps find another way to save Empusa. There is no other way to save Raquel."

"There is no other way to release someone from the Underworld but through me," Hades insisted. "This offer makes the most sense. And there is one last thing. It is true that Zeus can leave if the bloodstone stays. But surely you do not wish to leave it here unattended. If you do not stay with it, who will guard it? You must stay."

The silence was deafening.

"Just a moment," I said quietly and I walked woodenly to my husband. I pressed my forehead to his chest and allowed his arms to fold around me. I could feel every eye in the near vicinity on us, waiting to see what we would decide.

Cadmus lowered his head until his lips brushed my ear. "I will follow you anywhere," he said huskily. "My life is nothing without you in it. We should stay. The Isles are a paradise. We'll be happy there. We'll be together and that is all that matters. I think recent events have proven that."

I looked up, meeting his dark gaze. "Are you certain?" I whispered.

He nodded solemnly. "I've never been so certain."

I pressed a kiss to his lips. "I love you."

"And I love you."

I turned around. "Fine. We have a deal… on one condition. I want access to the portal that links to Zeus' palace on Olympus- the real Olympus. I want the ability to visit my parents in the Spiritlands."

Everyone shifted their gaze to Hades. He looked agreeable and a little smug as he nodded, his dark cloak curling around him in the breeze.

"Done. Just as I allow Persephone to return to Olympus to visit her mother, I will allow you the same privileges. See, I am not unreasonable."

I stared at him. "So that is it? It is done?"

He nodded. "So be it. It is so."

"There is one more thing," a voice called out. Everyone turned to see who had spoken. Ortrera stood proudly in front of her warriors.

"I would like permission to stay with Harmonia in the Isles."

I froze. "Ortrera, no! Why would you do that?"

She smiled faintly. "Because, dear sister. You are guarding a powerful weapon. Your pendant contains Zeus' own fate, which in turn affects that of the entire world. My warriors and I wish to help you guard it. And you, too, of course."

"Of course," I murmured. My sister wasn't much for sentiments.

Hades nodded, clearly pleased that he had gained more souls for the Underworld. "So be it."

And it was done. Negotiations were over.

I would've collapsed to the ground in a heap if it weren't for Cadmus' arms supporting me.

"It will be alright," he murmured to me. "I promise you."

I nodded. I knew that it would be. "Where's Raquel?" I whispered.

"She's at the palace on the Isles with Ahmose."

"Then let us go there."

He nodded and scooped me into his arms. Regardless of my decision to stay in the Underworld, I had never felt so safe. My husband's arms were the safest place in the world.

* * *

From the comfort of a chaise lounge, I watched Raquel scamper and play in the courtyards of the palace. The gardens were manicured and perfect here, and there was even an English maze for her to get lost in. I closed my eyes wearily. It had been hours since we had returned from Hades' palace, but I was still tired. My depression had taken my energy. Even sipping on nectar, it would take awhile to regain it fully. As I listened to Raquel's joyful laughter, I smiled.

"There is nothing as beautiful as a child, is there not?"

I opened my eyes to find Zeus next to me. I nodded. "You're right. She's a miracle."

He sat in the chair next to me and calmly observed my daughter playing.

"You have done well, Harmonia," he said quietly. "Every decision you make is laced with loyalty and responsibility. I am honored to have you part of my family."

I looked at him. Honored?

He read my mind and laughed.

"Of course, I am honored. I doubt there is anyone else who could have come through this as you did. Time and again, you have sacrificed yourself for the greater good and that is to be commended."

I nodded wordlessly. He had no idea how hard it had been.

"I must apologize, also," he said regretfully. "I do know how difficult it has been for you. And I'm sorry that I had to do it in the way that I did. But you see, I too have to consider others before myself. My decision, my plan, was formed to save us all. Many might see this last decision of yours as a punishment. I hope you do not.

"The Isles of the Blessed are indeed that. They are a paradise meant for only the purest of heart. You will live here for all of eternity in perfect bliss with your family. It is not a punishment at all, it is a reward. This palace will be yours. Raquel can run and play in paradise and you and Cadmus will never face another goodbye. It is a blessing."

His silver eyes beseeched mine. "Do you agree?"

I nodded. "I do think so. Cadmus and I have faced so much heartache. It is comforting to know that we will spend eternity in bliss."

"It will be so," Zeus assured me. "And I hereby renounce the curse on your bloodstone. With my words, it has been lifted."

I almost felt physically lighter as he said those words. "Thank you," I whispered.

"You're welcome. I owe you much. If there is ever anything that I can do for you, you only need ask."

"What of Empusa?" I asked suddenly, as her delicate face came unbidden into my mind. "Has Hecate found her?"

Zeus shook his head. "No, but she will. We do not know if Empusa realizes that she is free. If so, she may take flight to the mortal world. She is terrified that her father will find her and destroy her to prevent the curse's reversal. But wherever she is, trust that we will find her. I know that Hecate will tirelessly search for her."

I nodded, satisfied in that. Zeus rose from his chair, pausing for one moment with his hand silently on my shoulder before he retreated back into the palace. It wasn't long before my parents took his place.

"Are you certain that you wish to do this?" my mother demanded, her silver eyes concerned.

I laughed. "Well, the decision has been made. I certainly hope so!"

She shook her head wryly. "Harmonia, I..."

"We're proud of you," Ares interrupted. "You are the best daughter I could ever have dreamed of having. We are only a portal away, remember that."

A knot formed in my throat and I nodded quickly. "I know. And you can visit me here, as well."

"Trust me," my mother said. "I'll be here so much that you'll wonder if I'm ever going to leave." I laughed, but only because I knew it was true.

"Mother," I began. "Can you look in on my mortal mother from time to time to make sure she is alright?" My chest constricted at the thought of never seeing her again.

Aphrodite nodded solemnly. "I promise that I will. I'm going to keep an eye on my own mortal parents as well, along with my grandmother. Their memories have all been taken from them- it is as though we never existed. But that is for the best. Mortals cannot handle this sort of emotional upheaval."

"Oh, I think mortals are stronger than we give them credit for," I answered. "But in this case, you are right. It is best that they forget us. It's too painful to miss those that we love."

She nodded. "I love you, you know."

I hugged her tightly and Ares wrapped his arms around us both.

"You both act as though this is farewell," he growled. "It isn't. It is 'goodbye for now.' We'll be back to visit very soon."

I leaned up and kissed him on the cheek. "I love you, too, father."

He nodded silently and I noticed that his dark eyes were watery. I discreetly looked away. It wouldn't be polite to point out that the god of war was crying.

"You should go say goodbye to Raquel," I suggested. Ares nodded without looking at me and they set out across the courtyard to find her. I turned in time to find Cadmus slipping up behind me.

"Did we do the right thing?" I asked softly, reaching out to trace his face with my fingers. Together, we turned and gazed across our new backyard- it had an amazing view of the Isles of the Blessed. Everything was lush, green and tranquil here. It truly was a blissful paradise.

At the same time, we both breathed,"Yes."

Then we looked at each other and laughed.

"Do you realize that we'll never have to say goodbye again?" Cadmus asked, his chocolate eyes gentle. "We'll never have another last kiss."

My stomach clenched and then relaxed. He was right. Our heartache was behind us. I pulled him to me and kissed him fiercely, enjoying the way his heart beat next to mine. It was perfectly in sync, as a soul mate's should be.

"Then here is our first kiss of forever," I murmured against his lips.

He smiled against mine and we turned back to watch our daughter. Ares was carrying Raquel on his mighty shoulders and she leaned down to laugh into his ear. Aphrodite skipped alongside them, dainty and beautiful as they laughed. Their happiness was almost tangible and I felt as if I could reach out and touch it.

I was suddenly full of contentment and joy, as I should be. All would be right with the world, after all. As the goddess of peace, it was my job to ensure that the world was a happy, contented place. And I had learned that the only way to do that was to start with myself. As I grasped my husband's hand and watched my family approach, I knew that everything would be fine. Our love was lasting, our life was beautiful and our eternity was forever.

The End

# Author's Notes

This finale has been difficult for me to write. I love these characters and this is a goodbye of sorts. I won't spend every day with them now and that leaves me sad. But I'm happy as well. When I started, I wasn't entirely sure how their story would end and I am relieved that it ended on a joyful note.

In real mythological legend, Cadmus and Harmonia chose to leave Olympus and reside in Elyria. They had suffered so much misfortune because of Harmonia's cursed necklace (including tragic ends for their children) that they simply couldn't bear it any longer. They appealed to Zeus and so Zeus turned them into snakes and sent them to Elyria for all of eternity.

I couldn't bear to turn them to snakes. Who in the world would want to spend eternity with scales and eating live mice? Not my heroes! I think not.

Raquel is not an actual mythological figure. I thought that Cadmus and Harmonia deserved to have a child that not only survived with them, but flourished. Sure, she ended up dying, but her soul is alive and well with them in the Underworld now and they will live together, forever.

I like my version of their happily-ever-after so much better than actual legend and I hope you do, too. It was certainly fun to write. I didn't realize prior to this that the Underworld wasn't all fire and brimstone. It was fascinating to discover in my hours of research that it was an entire subterranean world.

And who knew that Hades was so sexy?

I hope that you have enjoyed following *The Bloodstone Saga*. I am sad to draw it to a close, but I am excited to announce that my next series, *The Moonstone Saga,* will follow Empusa, Hecate's daughter.

*Question:* If your mother is the goddess of witchcraft and your father is a soul-sucking vampire, what does that make you?

*Answer:* Cursed.

Empusa is vulnerable and beautiful, but she is also very, very dangerous. With all the beauty and charm of a Siren, but cursed as a blood-sucking succubus, Empusa longs for love and a normal life. Neither of these can ever be hers, because the only thing she brings to anyone she loves is death.

Her story is fascinating and I hope you will stick around for the ride. I have included the first chapter of my new series, *The Moonstone Saga,* for your reading enjoyment.

I need to take a moment and thank my beta readers. Melissa Blau and Ana H… thank you so much for reading the draft form of this book. Your input was invaluable. And Shari Kosowan, thank you. In addition to offering her insightful opinions, Shari kindly helped me polish up the Chosen One's prophecy. It sparkles now—thank you, Shari.

And to my readers: THANK YOU, THANK YOU for reading my work. I truly, truly appreciate it.

If you would like to read chapter one of my exciting new series,
*The Moonstone Saga,*
Please continue reading.

# *Soul Kissed*

## Chapter One

I see colors. Blurs of colors blend together in distorted shapes, vivid and muted, light and dark. This is what always happens and so I immerse myself in the familiarity of it now as I allow my eyes to un-focus. As my reality becomes a colorful haze around me, I know it is for the best. I don't want to stare into this man's eyes as I kill him.

With a quick breath, I inhale his life. Even though it is feeble and sick and hollow, I allow it to slide down my throat, expanding my lungs with what was left of his vitality. In all honesty, there wasn't much there. Cancer had sucked at him for years, taking his strength and his will to survive. But this little puff of life was enough for me. It would sustain me for a few weeks.

I opened my eyes just in time to find his own turning cloudy and I knew that he was gone. I straightened and gazed down at the man in the hospital bed, combing his blonde hair back with my fingers. He was slender and handsome, quiet and witty. I had truly liked him, as much as I dared to like anyone, anyway.

Divorced, 39-year old Daniel Delacorte. His daughter had died when she was only fifteen in a freak car accident. Apparently, she had been beautiful and vibrant and when she died, she took his will to live with her. And then at that most inopportune time, right when he was drowning in grief, he had been diagnosed with cancer.

He wouldn't have lasted much longer, even without my interference. Mortal lives were so often tragic. I had seen it in his eyes a few weeks back when I had bumped into him in the hospital halls. He was tired and he was ready to go. And then, because I reminded him of his daughter, he felt an instant connection with me. Little did he know that I would send him to meet her.

The door flew open and a team of nurses noisily shoved a crash cart in front of them.

"Move back," one of them ordered me as she yanked two paddles from an aging, yellowed machine.

Obligingly, I scooted against the wall. I felt nothing as I watched them work over Daniel's lifeless body, nothing as one of his hands dangled limply over the side of the bed. His fingers were pale. He had been too sick to go outdoors into the sunshine. I still felt nothing. I had been doing this for so long. I had long since learned to harden myself against what I had to do. If I didn't, I would go insane. To survive, I embraced the numbness.

A doctor tiredly loped through the doorway, barely glancing at Daniel. The nurses had been futilely working for several minutes now. I knew it was hopeless and apparently, this exhausted doctor did too.

"Time of death?" he asked the closest nurse, the one wearing faded puppy dog scrubs. Her face was pained as she glanced up, first at the doctor and then at the clock.

"5:03."

They stopped working and the doctor turned to me.

"I'm so sorry for your loss, miss. There is a chapel down the hall and we can call a chaplain for you, if you'd like."

I shook my head.

"That's not necessary. I only met Daniel a few weeks ago, here in the hospital. He didn't have anybody, so I started visiting him here…" my voice trailed off.

The doctor briefly assessed me with trained, weary eyes. I honestly think he was too tired to care what my relationship was to his patient. He clearly needed a good night's sleep. After a moment, he nodded.

"Well, if you change your mind—" But he was interrupted as the door swung open and a boy stood in the doorframe.

My first inclination was to think *boy*, but he was probably eighteen or so. After being around for a thousand years, all mortal men began to seem like boys to me. This one was handsome. Sandy blonde hair, warm hazel eyes, athletic tanned build. His eyes were pretty and they widened when he saw Daniel.

The doctor turned to him.

"I'm sorry, you shouldn't be in here."

The boy straightened his broad shoulders and thrust out his chin. "He's my uncle. I'm Brennan Delacorte."

I was surprised, but tried not to show it. Daniel hadn't mentioned any other family. He always talked about feeling alone because of the loss of his daughter. He was divorced and I honestly hadn't thought that he would leave a grieving family behind. I gulped and fought back guilt. I was definitely feeling something now and I didn't like it. This situation broke one of my own rules. I always aimed for men who would leave no one.

The doctor hurried to the boy. "I'm so sorry for your loss," he said quickly. "We did everything we could, but your uncle… well, I think he was just ready."

The boy nodded silently, his eyes frozen on his uncle.

"Are your parents with you?" the doctor asked. "You probably shouldn't be alone."

Brennan shook his head and swallowed, like he wanted to say something, but couldn't trust his voice. And I couldn't help myself. The vulnerable, sad look on his face combined with my rush of guilt did me in and the words were out before I could take them back.

"I'll stay with him."

Brennan's head whipped around and I realized that he hadn't even noticed that I was in the room. His eyes widened again, but this time in confusion. I could practically see the wheels turning in his head as he wondered who I was.

"My name's Em," I explained softly. "I met your uncle here at the hospital a while ago. He was a really nice person."

"Yes, he was." Brennan relaxed. I could see it as his shoulders un-tightened. It never ceased to amaze me. My presence was soothing to mortals, it drew them in. In reality, it should alarm them, put them on edge, cause them to run far, far away from me. But they never did.

The doctor nodded and took his leave, as the one lingering nurse straightened Daniel's blankets. With one last sympathetic gaze, she left Brennan and I alone.

I watched this boy curiously as he approached his dead uncle. It had been so long since I had allowed my heart to warm to something. I didn't like it that way, but it was simply the way things had to be. It was interesting to me now to watch the sadness flit across this boy's handsome features. I felt a small twinge, somewhere deep within me, but I ignored it.

"I didn't know him very well," Brennan said softly as he picked up Daniel's limp arm and replaced it next to his still body. "After his daughter died, he kind of withdrew from the world. He thought no one understood. He stopped talking to my dad, and everyone else for that matter, and life went on without him."

"I don't think that he really wanted to go on," I offered limply. What else could I say? *I'm sorry, but I just shortened your uncle's already terminal life because I needed his soul?* Yeah, that would be an icebreaker, for sure.

"I know. He's been like that ever since Kayla's accident."

Brennan gazed down at his uncle and I paused at the expression on his face. He was still loving, still reverent, even though Daniel had shut them all out in his grief. It was fascinating. Mortals were so different from those in my world. But then, I had a father who was trying to kill me. That might slant my views somewhat.

"Are you, er, sick, too?" Brennan asked me hesitantly as his hazel eyes skimmed over my body. I knew he was searching for the tell-tale sickly, sallow look of a cancer patient. I shook my head.

"No. I volunteer here. I read to children, sit with sick adults, stuff like that."

Appreciation flickered on his face and I unconsciously took a step back. *No. Do not like me,* I silently commanded him. Not that it would work. Men were always drawn to me. They couldn't help it. It was one of my gifts. Or a curse, depending on how you looked at it.

"That's a very nice thing for you to do," he acknowledged softly. I saw the attraction in his eyes and I took a sharp breath. For some reason, his warm, vulnerable gaze appealed to me and I wanted to tell him that I was dangerous, to stay away. But of course I couldn't.

"It's not a big deal," I said instead. "I like it."

That wasn't the truth. I didn't like being here, because I only came here when it was getting close to time to feed. The hospital was the perfect place to find people on death's door.

It was the only thing I could do to assuage my guilt, to placate my conscience. If I took the life of someone who was going to die anyway, it wasn't really killing them, was it? That's what I told myself anyway.

I looked through the empty doorway, half expecting more of his family members to show up. "Is your father coming?"

Brennan shook his head. "No. And he doesn't know that I'm here. The hospital called this morning to tell us that Daniel's situation was serious. But my dad wouldn't come. They had some bad blood at the end."

"That's really sad," I murmured. "Your uncle was a good person."

"I thought you didn't know him very well?" he raised an eyebrow questioningly.

"I didn't. I'm just good at gauging people. It's a gift." I shrugged my shoulders. It was easy to gauge someone when you drank their soul. But I didn't mention that part.

"My dad's a good person, too," Brennan said. "But they're both stubborn. They both said harsh things and neither of them would take them back. And sometimes, when that happens with family, it's worse than anything else, because you trusted them more to begin with. You know?"

He had no idea how well I knew. My own father had traded my soul for his freedom from the Underworld, transferring his hateful curse onto me. I definitely understood familial betrayal. I lived with it every day.

I nodded. "I know."

Brennan gave me a sheepish look. "I'm sorry for telling you these things. I don't know what's wrong with me. I think just seeing my uncle like this… it was a shock…"

I almost took a step forward and put my hand on his shoulder and that inclination startled me. I knew better. For anyone else, that would be a simple, harmless gesture. But not for me. I stayed where I was.

"I'm really sorry for your loss," I offered instead. "I know it's hard."

Brennan nodded wordlessly. He gazed at his uncle one more time before turning back to me. "Hey. Do you want to go down to the cafeteria and get a cup of coffee? I don't feel like going home just yet."

He was hesitant, but hopeful. Something about his voice reminded me of warm maple syrup. Warm and thick, yet somehow sexy at the same time. I felt the stirrings deep in my belly, the ones that urged me to step closer and inhale this man. I took another subconscious step back. Quickly.

"I can't," I answered. "I'm sorry."

He studied me for a moment, his head cocked. I had definitely been wrong. He wasn't a boy. He had the serious gaze of a man.

"Please?" he added. "I'd like to be with someone who spent time with Daniel at the end. I can't explain it. I just want to make sure that he was okay. I won't take much of your time, I promise. Just one cup of coffee."

I had more time than he could ever imagine. I was immortal. That was a fact I reminded myself of as I stared at this appealing man. Yes, he was handsome and sexy, but I could handle him. I could handle anything. My mother was the goddess of witchcraft, for Pete's sake- the most powerful witch in the world. Some of that had to have rubbed off on me.

I finally nodded. "Alright. Just one cup."

He smiled and I could swear the room brightened. I appraised his face quickly. Why was I drawn to him? I wasn't hungry. Physically, he was handsome. Rugged features, healthy, vibrant coloring. My pulse buzzed in my wrist, quick and feather-light. I swallowed hard. I didn't normally do this. There was no point. But for once, I listened to my heart, not my head. It would be nice to not be lonely for a few minutes.

Brennan held the door for me and I slipped past him, careful not to touch him. As I passed, though, I inhaled. He smelled delicious, like sunshine and man.

He punched at the elevator button and we waited, him patiently, me not-so-much. I had grown to hate the smell of hospitals, that sterile, medicinal smell, and I wanted to leave here. Now. My purpose here was done and I wouldn't have to come back for a few weeks.

With a melodic 'ding', the metal doors opened and Brennan gestured me forward.

"Your chariot," he smiled.

I couldn't help but smile back. He had such an easy, laid back way about him. His spirit seemed… almost gentle. And that seemed strange because he was so huge. I hadn't realized how enormous he was until we stepped into the elevator and I saw our reflections. The top of my head was only chest-high to him.

As we glided downward to the main floor, I discreetly looked at him in the mirror. He really was handsome. Broad, muscular shoulders, sandy blonde hair that just started to flip upward at his neckline. It made him look a little mischievous. Warm hazel eyes that seemed almost like butterscotch and… were looking directly at me. He raised an eyebrow and I looked away quickly. He had totally just caught me giving him the once-over. Drat. That was the last thing I needed right now.

The doors slid open and he held out his arm.

"After you," he said quietly.

His voice was husky and I found myself wishing I could take a bath in it. It was gentle and sexy at the same time. As soon as I had the thought, I wanted to slap myself. What in the name of the gods was wrong with me? I had never been so affected by a mortal. Not ever.

As I stepped past him, he moved slightly and I bumped into him. Our forearms collided, the length of my arm from wrist to elbow pressed against him. White hot electricity jolted through me and I exhaled sharply, the breath seemingly forced from my lungs as my fingertips tingled. Brennan inhaled at the same time, his eyes slightly unfocused from the contact.

*Shit.*

His aura appeared to me, a vivid array of colors and my breath froze in my throat, my lips automatically opening just a bit. His energy was delicious, sweet and pure, and I was hard-pressed to pull away. I felt an almost uncontrollable need to draw nearer to him, just a little.

*I can handle it.* My own thoughts betrayed me.

Before I could help myself, I stepped closer…like a moth to a flame. My lips hovered just a couple of inches from his and we lingered there, like we were the only two people in the world, drawn together by an invisible ribbon of energy. My heart took off like helicopter blades and I felt it thrumming in my chest, louder with each beat.

His hazel eyes stared into mine, the flecks of gold shining in the dim light of the elevator. I tried to focus, to concentrate on his eyes rather than the incredible pull that I felt toward him as I fought to gather the strength to move. I just needed to move away. It shouldn't be so hard.

But as I tried to will my feet to move, Brennan reached out his fingers and touched mine.

Sensations I'd never felt before, as soft as velvet but as strong as steel, flooded through my body, filling every vein, lifting me like I was floating on swelling waves. It was exquisite, unique and petrifying.

"What the hell…" Brennan murmured, his eyes still frozen to mine. His voice was quiet and raspy and filled with wonder, but it was enough to break my fixation on him and I yanked away from him and lunged out of the elevator.

"Wait!" he called to me. But I was already running down the hall. I had to get away from him. Far, far away before I hurt him. Curious nurses moved out of my way as I ran and I didn't look back even though Brennan was still calling my name.

I took the nearest exit, throwing the door open so hard that it slammed into the cinderblocks behind it. I dove beneath the stairs and collapsed into a heap in the corner, sucking in air. *What the hell was that?* I had never felt that way before in my life.

Typically, when I fed, I started the process at my will. It was a conscious effort, something that I could easily control. My self-restraint was never tested. It was just like kissing. I simply brushed my lips against theirs and sucked their souls right out of their bodies. It was quick and painless.

But with Brennan… I certainly had no intentions of stealing his soul, yet his aura had appeared with just my touch. He was young and vibrant and alive…and I wanted him. I wanted him like I had never wanted anything else in my life. My need for him had filled me up, distracted me, overwhelmed me. I had never felt a connection like that before

It was startling.

Amazing.

Terrifying.

Because it was incredible. Emotion had flooded my body, pulsing through my heart… waking it from an ever-long slumber. And because of that, I could never see him again. My curse made me dangerous.

I killed everyone that loved me.

To read more of Em and Brennan,
Please read *Soul Kissed,* the first exciting book in *The Moonstone Saga.*
Available on Amazon and Barnes and Noble.com

www.ingramcontent.com/pod-product-compliance
Lightning Source LLC
Chambersburg PA
CBHW050931120626
46552CB00001B/153

* 9 7 8 0 6 1 5 5 7 4 6 5 3 *